DESCENDANTS OF EVIL

David James

ROMAN *Books*
www.roman-books.co.uk

Copyright © 2011 David James

ISBN 978-93-80905-24-2

Typeset in Adobe Garamond Pro

First published in 2011
Paperback Edition 2012

1 3 5 7 9 8 6 4 2

British Library Cataloguing in Publication Data.
A catalogue record for this book is available from the British Library.

ROMAN *Books*
26 York Street, London W1U 6PZ, United Kingdom
2nd Floor, 38/3, Andul Road, Howrah 711109, WB, India
www.roman-books.co.uk | www.roman-books.co.in

Printed and bound in India by
Roman Printers Private Limited
www.romanprinters.com

DESCENDANTS OF EVIL

d James was born and brought up in Wales. He currently
in Carmarthenshire with his wife. *Descendants of Evil* is his
ut novel.

DESCENDANTS OF EVIL

ONE

On a bright, cold day in early October after a dry spell; a gusty wind blew the dust of the London streets into the face of Sir Roger Evesham. He stood, immaculately dressed in frock-coat and silk top-hat, on a pavement outside Waterloo Station.

Seeing an unoccupied passing hansom, he stepped forward and raised his cane to hail the cab. He had an appointment to see the prime minister, William Gladstone, at eleven, and it was already ten-thirty. The trains up from East Sussex, via Edenbridge, had been awkward and, to his chagrin, he now had to face the possibility of being a little late.

When the hansom came to a standstill about twenty feet beyond the point where he stood, the cabby turned to look at him enquiringly. Roger smiled up at him, wished him a 'good-morning' walked to the cab and got in.

When he had closed the doors and gathered the skirts of his coat around his legs to his satisfaction, he rapped with his cane on the trap above his head. The cabby lifted it, asked for his destination, and when he had been given it, clucked at the horse to set it in motion.

The tide of traffic thickened as they approached Downing Street and it seemed to Roger that the number of cabs, carts, wains, wagons, vans and Thomas Tilling omnibuses got greater and greater with every successive visit to the capital.

Roger found that, as they got nearer and nearer to Downing Street, his palms became decidedly moist, despite the chill which comes with sitting motionless in an open vehicle on a cold day. He swallowed more than he usually did, too, probably in anticipation of the prospect of speaking clearly and intelligibly to the prime minister. He didn't want to take up too much of his valuable time. He struggled to fight off a strong impulse to run his fingers through his carefully groomed hair.

At length, they drew up outside Number Ten; Roger paid the cabby and descended. He gave the policeman on duty his letter from the prime minister who, after glancing at it, knocked to alert the doorman, who, after opening the door and also glancing at the letter showed Roger to a seat in an anteroom and took his hat and gloves.

This room contained a desk at which the prime minister's private secretary sat bent over some documents; he looked briefly at Roger, and then went on with his work. Hushed voices from the inner sanctum told Roger that he had not inconvenienced the prime minister, unduly; an interview was clearly still in progress.

After about five minutes, the door to the prime minister's office opened and two rather crestfallen gentlemen came out, closing the door behind them. They passed through the anteroom without looking up and quickly disappeared.

The prime minister's door opened again almost immediately and the man himself called for Sir Roger, who got to his feet and entered. As he turned away from closing the door, to face the prime minister, he involuntarily took a deep, but silent, intake of breath.

Gladstone, standing behind his desk, shook Roger's hand and sat down, indicating a chair on the opposite side for Roger as he did so.

As a preamble, Gladstone commiserated with him about the death of his father, congratulated him on his recent graduation *summa cum laude* from Oxford and then, after clearing his throat, came to the reason for his being summoned.

"As you are no doubt aware, your late father with his

remarkable acumen and penetrating insight was often helpful to the government of the day in the solution of several difficulties which this country faced.

Not a few of these would have gravely compromised our national security, if they had not been nipped in the bud by his clever elucidation," he said.

Roger nodded, gravely.

"I realise that you are still a very young man and that perhaps it is not right to expect you to follow in his footsteps quite so soon after Oxford, but your success there has reassured me about one thing which is of paramount importance: you are your father's son and show the same promise. I shall be frank with you, Roger; I have come across a little problem of exactly the kind which would have led me to consult your father."

Gladstone leaned back slightly in his chair as if to evaluate the other's reaction to this piece of information and it seemed to Roger that a trace of anxiety fleetingly crossed the older man's face. "Is there anything you would like to tell me?" he said very softly.

Roger realised that he was being appealed to, and that a great deal rested on his response; hence Gladstone's anxiety. Roger also realised that he had two clear options: he could agree with the prime minister that he was too young, leave, and probably never be anything other than a country squire. Or he could stay, discover what the problem was, find a solution by the grace of God, and continue in his father's footsteps. It was a veritable turning point in his life, but, in the light of certain unhappy events which had occurred to him since coming down from Oxford, he did not hesitate; he badly needed something to distract him.

"I would be honoured to accept your commission whatever it might be," he said.

Gladstone became perceptibly less tense. "Very well, but if

you seem to be getting into deep waters you must tell me at once, I would excuse you and appoint someone older and more experienced, albeit less gifted. I do not want you to come to any harm whatsoever; my conscience would not stand for it."

"I am at your service."

Gladstone leaned back in his chair and tented his hands on the desk. "What I tell you now must be regarded as most secret."

"It goes without saying."

"A week ago a strange series of events took place on the south coast which culminated in a man's death. This man, who was dressed as a gentleman, was arrested by customs officials very early one morning, shortly after high tide, rolling a barrel of gunpowder up a track which led from the beach to his isolated cottage.

"When he was arrested, he did not put up any kind of fight, nor would he speak one word about his suspicious behaviour, and so he was locked up in the cells of a police station situated in a nearby town.

"Later that same day, after his cottage had been searched, the inspector and sergeant went to the cells in the hope that he might prove more talkative, but discovered him lying on the floor of his cell quite dead. A small glass phial which still bore traces of potassium cyanide lay beside the body."

"Did the police find anything in the cottage which might throw some light on the mystery?"

"Very little, apart from an additional two barrels of gunpowder. The only other item of interest was this." Gladstone unlocked a drawer next to him and placed a small, expensively-bound book on the desk.

Roger took up the book and opened it at random, what met his eye were two examples of the most appalling doggerel; yet they, and the rest of the equally bad collection, he saw as he turned the pages, were printed on good quality paper using violet ink. No author's name appeared anywhere in the book, nor those of the publisher or printer.

He looked up with what must have been a quizzical expression on his face and saw the same sentiments reflected in the face of the prime minister.

"Yes," said Gladstone, nodding in agreement with his unasked question, "why would anyone take so much trouble and expense to publish such rubbish?"

"It must have been privately published," said Roger, "perhaps, for the sake of pure vanity or swank."

"I absolutely agree with you," said the prime minister, "but, I must leave any speculation and weighing up of facts to you, so that you can report back to me with your findings, later."

"I shall certainly do so," said Roger.

"I want you to look thoroughly into this matter, it may be that it will come to nothing, but in these troubled times one cannot afford to take any chances. Please take the book and this police report of the incident with you," he said, taking a folder out of the same drawer which had contained the book of poetry and handing it to Roger. "Please also accept this with my compliments," he went on, handing Roger a handsome black-leather briefcase which he took from somewhere behind his desk.

Roger stood and opened the briefcase to place the items which he had been given inside and saw something metal gleaming at the bottom. He looked up to see Gladstone looking at him with a smile.

"That is your gold insignia of office as an agent of this government. It entitles you to travel anywhere and into any place in the British Isles, and indeed, The Empire, without let or hindrance from any official, while carrying out secret work vital to Her Majesty's Government. You can also use the authority vested in you, by me, as a bearer of the insignia, to commandeer any personnel and resources you deem necessary in an emergency. Your father was given one which was exactly similar. And now, I really must say good-bye and Godspeed. I am afraid that I have a pressing engagement at eleven-thirty."

They shook hands and Roger departed with a little bow.

When he had regained the street, Roger realised that Gladstone had not mentioned his erstwhile fiancée, Lady Amelia Hindthorpe. He must, then, have heard about her affair with Charles.

TWO

Roger decided to dine at the Café Royal before returning home. There were three reasons for this: he was surprisingly hungry; he loved the Café Royal because of its associations with famous and infamous people; and last but not least, he wanted to be alone for a time to mull over everything the prime minister had told him and one of the private dining rooms at the Café Royal was admirably suited to that purpose. He had to admit, however, that the private rooms were all almost invariably taken by couples of one kind or another, who had more than dining in mind. No matter.

His resolve to dine in private disappeared when he saw that Sanderson was sitting in one of the chairs set aside for those waiting for a table. He had a momentary impulse to withdraw, but before he could do so Sanderson saw him and signalled that he should join him; so that they could dine together. It was the very last thing he wanted: Sanderson knew all about Amelia and Charles and, as a recent encounter with him had shown, he was not averse to talking at length about the subject.

"Hello, my dear Evesham, how do you do?" Sanderson rose to greet him holding out his hand.

"Very well, Sanderson, thank you," said Roger, giving the standard reply.

"Would you care to join me for luncheon?"

"I would be delighted," said Roger, with a thin smile. I would not, he thought, privately.

"I am next in line for a private room," Sanderson continued.

Oh no! I don't believe it, thought Roger. He could hardly

believe his bad luck. It was pretty awful to have to dine with Sanderson, whose insensitivity to the finer feelings was legendary; it was another thing again to have to dine with him in a confined space. "How nice!" he exclaimed aloud.

At that moment the head waiter told Sanderson that his room was ready, and Roger, whose cup of misery was almost full, followed the two men to the private room.

At first, the luncheon proceeded without much conversation, both men being engrossed in their food, but, soon after they had finished their respective main courses, the topic which Roger simply did not wish to discuss with anyone was broached by Sanderson, exactly as he had feared.

"Do you see much of that nice young lady of yours, these days?" enquired Sanderson. "Decent looking gel," he went on, rubbing salt into the wound.

Roger marvelled at the ineptness of these remarks, but remembered that Sanderson was also noted for not having much in the way of a retentive memory, or for that matter, much in the way of an intellect. If it had not been for these factors and the fact that they had been at Oxford together, he would have risen from the table and walked out. Indeed, if this luncheon had been taking place a century earlier he would have taken Sanderson's remarks as an insult and challenged him to a duel. As it was, he simply replied, "no" in as colourless a tone as possible, in the hope that Sanderson would perceive his lack of interest and, like a normal person, sense his deep reluctance to discuss his erstwhile fiancée and veer sharply away from the subject, or better still become silent until the meal was concluded.

For a time, after this, Sanderson was silent and Roger's hope that that was the end of his ordeal began to rise a little.

"Oh, wait a minute," said Sanderson, looking up from his pudding and waving his spoon for emphasis, "I remember now, there was some unpleasantness or other concerning her, wasn't there?"

Roger felt a pressure in his head and for some seconds debated with himself whether he should allow a considerable string of expletives to flow from his tongue, of which 'chump' would be about the kindest, when he realised that he was dealing with something with which he had not a great deal of experience: a congenital idiot. One must always make allowances for idiots, he thought. On the other hand, he didn't suffer fools gladly. This conflict of ideas caused the pressure in his head to increase. He removed the napkin from his lap, carefully folded it and placed it on the tablecloth next to his plate.

"I must go now. I have a headache and must get some fresh air. Thank you for the luncheon. You must allow me to be your host on another occasion. Good-bye." And with that, Roger picked up his hat, gloves and cane and departed.

The memory of Sanderson's utterly astonished stare stayed with him for some little time, as his cab weaved its way to the station. Soon, more pressing matters drove this image from his consciousness as the stopping train slowly made its way back to East Sussex and Roger's home at Evesham Meads, he pondered on the strange story of the gunpowder smuggler. The prime minister, in Roger's view, was right to be so concerned. If a man would prefer to kill himself rather than explain his actions, it seemed likely that there was much about the affair that was hidden at the present time, and it also hinted at something very dark.

Roger leant back against the cushions of the seat and lit a cigar to aid his thinking. The compartment was empty and he was glad of that, he did his best thinking when completely alone.

After turning the facts around in his mind for twenty minutes or so, without forming any real conclusions, he had to give the problem up for the moment. He would spend some time that evening writing down everything that occurred to him.

At that moment the train left a wood and entered the river valley which ran between his estate and that of Lord Hindthorpe, the actual boundary being the meandering river, itself.

He remembered his father telling him that the building of the railway, in 1846, had caused a dispute with the railway company and a rift between the Hindthorpes and the Eveshams which had taken some years to heal.

The dispute had arisen because neither family had wanted the tracks to be laid on their land. In the end, an uneasy agreement between the two families and the company had been arrived at, whereby the line was laid more or less equally on the adjoining estates, criss-crossing the river several times; but the truth was that this pleased neither family. This agreement was reached only a few weeks before the Act of Parliament made the progress of the work on the line mandatory, it was the best that could be made of a bad job.

Eventually, in the fullness of time, both sides saw sense; the two families were not really angry with each other; rather, they were angry with a common enemy: the railway company for proposing the idea in the first place. Once this idea had been accepted, peace reigned between the families, once more, and they had remained on the best of terms ever since. Roger shook his head, smiling to himself. The whole thing seemed so silly, now, but at the time it had been deadly serious.

Soon, he was able to look out of the carriage window and see the stately pile on the other side of the valley which was the home of Lord Hindthorpe, his wife, and his only daughter Lady Amelia. Thinking of this gave him a sharp pang. Lady Amelia had, until about three months ago, been his fiancée and the thing which caused him the most pain was the fact that they had been sweethearts since childhood. He was tense, now, and sat on the edge of his seat, drawing hard at his cigar and inhaling deeply.

It was obviously going to be some time before he got over her and her affair with the French nobleman Charles. Charles had been his best friend when they were up at Oxford together and that rankled, too, very much so.

At last, the train pulled into the village station of Hindthorpe and Roger opened the compartment door and descended onto the platform; he was very glad the journey was over and that he could soon be alone with his pain, like a wounded animal.

He had asked Jessup, his phlegmatic coachman, to meet every train down from London after midday and there he sat on the high seat of the second-best brougham like a man with a secret sorrow. He touched his cockaded hat when he saw Roger and got down to open and close the door of the carriage for him. Roger made himself comfortable and rapped on the window with his cane. There came a sudden jolt and they were off. Jessop had been taught, like the best coachmen, that it was not done to use verbal commands to his horses, and so he simply gave the horse a flick on one shoulder with his whip to start and one on the other shoulder when he wanted to stop. He had spent much time and energy teaching this trick, among others, to the horses in his care.

When they reached the foot of the steps which led to the front door, Roger's only dog, Ralphy the old Bedlington terrier, the last of several and one who had been a great favourite of his father, came slowly and painfully down the steps to greet him; his tail gently wagging. "Good boy," said Roger, after he got down from the carriage, taking off his right glove to more properly fondle his ears and pat his woolly back. "Good old Ralphy." Ralphy was unfortunately deaf and it was said in the servants' hall that the last trump, even, would not rouse him from his slumber.

Roger and the dog watched as the carriage departed for the

coach-house and then climbed up the steps together. Roger went indoors leaving the poor old dog on the top step to enjoy the last of the day's sunshine. He recalled that, when he was a boy of three, he had caused his father and mother some amusement by his insistence on calling the dogs 'bed linen terriers'.

After his valet had taken his coat, hat and gloves, Roger locked his briefcase in the safe in his study and then went upstairs to see his elderly and bedridden mother. His father had died four years before, when he had been twenty-two, and he, as his only son and heir became the twelfth baronet.

He opened her door quietly in case she was asleep. She turned her lace-capped head towards him and smiled at him when he entered her bedroom and extended her hand to him, as she always did. He took her withered and mottled hand and kissed her vellum-like cheek.

"How was your visit to town, Roger" she enquired, "did you meet any nice young ladies?"

"No Mamma I did not," he said, gently. His mother almost always asked him this question whenever he went anywhere, other than somewhere on the estate and sometimes even then, and she always slightly emphasised the word 'nice', it was her way of showing her disapproval of Amelia and her behaviour.

He was glad of her solidarity, but sometimes wondered if she would ever tire of the habit; presumably only when he actually did find a nice young lady. He was not actively seeking any at the moment; he felt much too raw and bloody, as if some part of him had been torn out by force.

That evening, Roger dined alone in the small dining room; the large dining room, better known below stairs as the Great Hall, was only used when he had several guests for dinner.

This room was haunted by the ghost of Lady Amelia, and as Roger gazed down the long table towards the mullioned lead-glass windows at the far end of the room, he could almost see her misty silhouette seated opposite him. How often she had dined here with him! How happy they had been then! His eyes became blurry with tears.

For many weeks after the annulment of their betrothal he had not been able to dine in this room, the memories were far too painful; instead, he had dined in his private apartments.

He had even felt, in the days which followed their estrangement, that he would not be able to go on living at Evesham Meads, she was in every room of the house except his private rooms and bedroom. But, on the very morning when he had been about to announce his departure for Italy for a few months to stay with his cousin Sir Alfred Chivers, who had a villa in Florence, it occurred to him that he was being driven from his ancestral home by Lady Amelia and he rebelled against the notion and remained.

After he had dined, Roger repaired to his study to smoke a cigar or two and read the police report on the gunpowder smuggler and his suicide.

He unlocked the safe and removed the briefcase; from it he took the poetry book and the police report, which was very brief. It, very naturally, did not form any conclusions or opinions, save one, and confined itself to the few facts of the case. It listed the possessions of the dead man but these, apart from the poetry book and the barrels of gunpowder had been commonplace; some writing materials; a few unspecified newspapers; shaving tackle; pipes and tobacco; a few changes of clothing and so on. All the dead man's possessions had been of good quality and he had presented every appearance of being a gentleman when he was arrested. His accent when he spoke at all, which had been very little, had been that of a gentleman.

The dead man, who lived there under the name of William Thomas Rayleson, had only taken the cottage for three months and had been there just over two when arrested. This name and the previous address he had given to the landlord before taking up residence had both been false.

There was one curious thing noted by the inspector—the rent for three months had been paid in advance—a very unusual circumstance. Almost certainly, this had been done so that the weekly collection of rent, with the attendant risk of his true motives being discovered, had been obviated for the whole period.

The police inspector speculated that the smuggling of powder had been going on for the whole of the time the man was a tenant and that, perhaps, a considerable quantity had passed through his hands; where this possible stockpile was now could only be a matter for conjecture, the inspector added; the sole example of anything resembling an opinion.

Nobody had seen anything suspicious in the approximately two months before the police investigation got under way; the man was seldom out and about in the locality except to buy essentials from a few local shops. He was known in the locality as an amateur historian, but no one, when questioned by police officers, knew exactly how or why this was believed. He had lived as a recluse who had not sought the acquaintance of anyone and had covered his tracks very well.

The phial which had contained the cyanide bore no label and could throw no light on the investigation. Here, the report ended.

Roger next looked at the book of poetry; if indeed, he observed, the doggerel within deserved the name. As had been noted, the book had been expensively produced and consisted of sixty-two pages and sixty-two poems, one to each page. Under the last poem in the book, someone, possibly the dead man, had drawn, using coloured inks, a bright orange horseshoe with twelve nail-holes done in red.

On another page, under a poem, Roger found two three-figure numbers which had been written in pencil and then imperfectly erased. There was a greasiness on the page associated with these numbers which led him to believe that a makeshift eraser made from compressed bread had been used.

He noted that the vocabulary used in the construction of the poems was fairly basic with very few flowery or high-flown words, or those of more than three syllables; there was also very little repetition of nouns so that a certain amount of economy had been used in the printed matter of the book, an economy which was not reflected in the production of the book, itself.

But what, if anything, did these facts imply? Roger asked himself, but not aloud. He was a great believer in actually asking himself questions to which he required answers. He had discovered that if he did not, then very often no answers would come; this technique was as effective in his day-to-day life as it had been in the examination room, having been impressed upon him, when he was very young, by his father. He lit another cigar and leaned back in his chair with his eyes closed.

Dimly, at first, and then more clearly, he began to form the idea that the book had been, and probably still was being, used for the encoding of secret messages; in which case, there must be at least one other copy of the book and probably several. This would also explain the simplicity and economy of the words in the poems—they encompassed the basic vocabulary which was used in telegraphic communications.

He expected the messages to use, like all codes involving books, groups of three numbers to represent each word: the first number referring to the page; the second to the line; the third to the number of the word in that line.

But, if he was right, where did those messages appear? Somewhere public and easily accessible, otherwise there was no need for secrecy. In the personal column of a newspaper, then. Yes, but which paper and at what intervals of time?

He recalled seeing one or two curious numerical messages in the personal columns of at least one London paper fairly recently, but, because they had meant nothing to him at the time, he could not now remember which one, or how long ago.

Like his father before him, Roger preserved copies of three important London newspapers, on a daily basis, and then sent them, yearly, to a bookbinder in London to be bound into large volumes which were then archived in his library. Perhaps, if he looked through the piles of recent copies he would be able to find a sample of the number code in order to test his theory concerning the poetry book?

It was late, but he was determined to find at least one example of the numerical messages he recalled seeing; accordingly he made his way to the library where, luckily there was still some fire in the grate. He lit the lamps and brought the last few months' copies of *The Times*, *The Evening News* and *The Standard* to one of the reading tables, then he seated himself and began to examine the personal columns of *The Standard*, starting with the most recent editions and working back through the rest.

After the best part of an hour, he had established that no such messages had formed any part of its personal columns during the last six months. He heard the long-case clock in the front vestibule of the house strike midnight, but remained determined to press on with the search.

At length, again starting with the most recent editions, he found an example of the numerical messages in a Wednesday copy of *The Evening News* which was only two weeks old:

1,22,9,20,18,9,15,12;52,30,5;49,14,2;1,20,15,14,19.

He could hardly contain his disappointment and chagrin. The message did not consist of groups of three numbers as he had surmised; instead, the first group consisted of eight numbers and the last contained five; assuming that the semicolons were being used to separate each word.

However, the two middle groups contained three numbers each and he looked up the appropriate pages, lines, and number of words on a line and found the words: 'arrived' and 'ten', which, fetching pen and paper, he duly jotted down. It was not much to show for his labours, thus far, he reflected, lighting yet another cigar.

He sat in one of the fireside armchairs and smoked a good half of his cigar before he realised that he had not looked at Page One to see what, if any, significance it held. He jumped up and went to the table where the newspaper still lay open at the personal column. He noted at once that Page One was quoted as the page of reference in both the first and last group of numbers. But, in the book of poems, Page One simply consisted of twenty-six lines of a child's *aide-memoire* along the lines of 'A is for apple', 'B is for ball' etc. He went back to the armchair and slumped down to finish his cigar. He was beginning to feel the first intimations of tiredness and would have to call it a day if he was to see his estate manager at eight the next morning, as he did every day save Sunday. It seemed he would have to sleep on the problem.

He got up and began to blow out the lamps until only the one on the reading table was burning; this he took up and carried to the door, it would serve to light him to his bedroom. He locked the library door so that it would not be disturbed by the servants in the morning, washed and went to bed.

He woke when it was still pitch-dark and the solution to the problem of the night before, or rather, earlier that same day, flooded into his mind. He cursed himself for not seeing it before as he leaped out of bed, lit his bedside candle, and went downstairs in his dressing gown and nightgown holding the candle before him to light his way; it cast long, flickering shadows which reflected his anxiety and agitation. Luckily, it was still too early for the servants; otherwise he would have had to waste time by dressing fully.

It was really so very simple, if he was right; Page One was a special page which was used for words which did not appear in the text of the book. A group of numbers preceded by number one referred to the numerical order of letters in the alphabet.

A few minutes' work at the reading table confirmed this idea; the eight-number group was decoded as the word 'vitriol' and the five-letter group was decoded as the word 'tons', so that the complete message now read: 'vitriol arrived ten tons'.

The difficulty now was that the message meant nothing to him. Perhaps, the decoding of other messages might give him some clues. But, now, he had to lock the door and hasten back to his room before the servants began their morning duties; he did not want them to see him so dishevelled and improperly dressed.

THREE

Roger was drowsy and out of sorts as he went through the business of the day with his estate manager, but he managed to conceal it well, he believed. Luckily, there was nothing very taxing that morning and he was soon left to his own devices.

He had breakfasted at seven, his usual time, but he had had to force himself to eat, his appetite still marred by his only partial success of the night's work, together with the sleeplessness engendered by burning the candle at both ends.

He had several letters to write, and considered sending a preliminary report of his results, thus far, to the prime minister but decided against it. It was too risky, if it fell into the wrong hands it might precipitate a more rapid execution of whatever was afoot; it was for word-of-mouth communication, only. He realised, for the first time, that he now believed that something very sinister was being set in motion.

After he had finished writing his letters, he rang for his butler, Thompson, and gave him the letters to post.

After he had departed, Roger reflected that Thompson would place the letters in a special blue, canvas bag, then give them to the under-butler, Murdoch, who would then ring for Jessup to take him to the village post office where he would post them and buy stamps to the same value, this was Roger's idea and it meant that he never ran out of stamps.

Soon, Roger heard the carriage clattering down the drive *en route* for the village and he rose from his desk and looked out of the window in time to see the brougham disappearing through the distant gates.

He left his study and went to the library, outside the door of which were three of the downstairs maids in a state of obvious distress, a polished brass coal-scuttle containing the makings of a fire stood nearby. When they saw him approach they composed themselves and he saw one, presumably their spokeswoman, take a few steps towards him to meet him.

"If you please, sir," said this maid, "the library is locked and we've can't get in to dust it and such."

"That's quite all right," said Roger kindly, "it was I who locked it, and I don't want it attended to today. You three can give it an extra special dusting, and such, tomorrow, instead." He was adept at using the terminology of the servants without being patronising. The three maids bobbed a curtsey in unison, two of them picked up the coal-scuttle between them, and they all hurried away, with a frou-frou of skirts, bent on some other task. Roger unlocked the door and went inside. The fire was not lit, of course, and he would have to draw the curtains himself, but he was anxious to get on with the task in hand and didn't want to be disturbed.

He seated himself at the table and went on looking through copies of *The Evening News*. He found only two other messages, even though he went back through copies from the last six months. One, of three weeks ago, referred to 'tar coated barrels' and the other, more than two months old, to 'a meeting of the brotherhood on the twelfth'.

A search through copies of *The Times* going back six months discovered no further messages. He resolved to peruse the personal column of every copy of *The Evening News* from now on, despite the fact that the messages were cryptic and did not really advance his investigation very much.

He left the table and went to the south-facing window. He stood there for some time looking out; it was a lovely Indian-summer day with a slight breeze, but he was not really looking

26

at the view, he was turning his findings over in his mind.

After a time, he fell to wondering if the task the prime minister had set him was beyond his competence. No! That was no way to think, he had to succeed, and there was no other option. His father, who had solved many obscure problems for the government had always said that, without of course taking him into his confidence about the specific nature of the work he was engaged upon. He had loved his father and had been loved in turn by him. At that moment, because he felt so very alone, he missed him more than usual and he sank into a nearby armchair still thinking about him. The trouble was that thinking about people whom he had loved, and been loved by, set him thinking about Amelia.

Everybody had always said that he and Amelia were made for one another and he had always felt that she was his other half and had often told her so. She had just as often said as much to him, but recent events had demonstrated that her words were no longer true; perhaps they never had been. Her head had been turned by the handsome young Count Charles de Braquelin and it had proved to be mutual love at first sight.

Thinking about this was unbearably painful for him, but he could not help it. He seemed not to have the power of detachment he needed to stop thinking about her and pick up the pieces of his life and move on. Not yet, anyway. Perhaps, one day, he would have that power.

This illustrated the reason why he so welcomed the work set him by the prime minister, it was just what he needed to take his mind from Amelia and her French lover. He involuntarily bared his teeth in a sardonic smile. He could and would throw himself into the solution of this problem and would lay down his life if necessary. In any case, he seemed to be walking a narrow line between wanting to live and wanting to die.

Despite his resolution not to think about Amelia, some

perverse part of his mind would not allow him to dismiss her without at least one recollection.

He closed his eyes, as he remembered as if it were yesterday, the first time he met her... It was one of those sunny, breezy days in March with low clouds scudding across a bright blue sky and like many another ten year old boy he had decided to climb trees that afternoon. His favourite tree, a sycamore, stood on the other side of the river which formed the boundary line between his family's land and that of the Hindthorpes. This presented no difficulties concerning trespass because his father and Lord Hindthorpe were on very good terms and he was allowed to roam over most of the Hindthorpe estate.

Accordingly, he crossed the river using the stepping stones, then the fences and single-track railway line which ran on the Hindthorpe estate at this point and went to the tree.

One of the best things about this particular tree was that the upper branches made an excellent vantage point from which to observe the passing trains. There were not more than a dozen or so a day, travelling in both directions, so that he sometimes sat on a branch near the top of the tree for what seemed like hours without seeing more than one.

He was wearing a Norfolk jacket and knickerbockers which were ideal wear for this kind of activity because they were tight-fitting and less likely to snag on the branches.

As he climbed, he became aware that he was being observed, because the tree was not yet in leaf, from about a hundred yards distance, by a little girl in a black dress with a white smock over it and a young woman in a green dress; both wearing straw boaters.

The little girl left her companion, who was probably her governess, and ran to the foot of the tree, where she addressed him, with an upturned face, using a surprisingly imperious voice for someone so young.

"Little boy, come down from that tree, it doesn't belong to you and you are trespassing."

He had been about to say something very rude to her when he realised that she must be Lady Amelia, the daughter of Lord Hindthorpe. He had never met her; he had heard she was an invalid who was never allowed outside the house.

Despite her presence and admonitions, he was determined to reach the top of the tree and kept climbing until he did. Below, the little girl made growling noises of vexation because her person, and especially her hat, was being sprinkled by debris from the tree due to his body making contact with the branches and trunk, as he climbed.

"I'll fetch one our gamekeepers," she said, with her voice raised, now that he was further up the tree, "and he will shoot you if you don't come down." By this time, she had been joined by her governess who also stared upwards at him.

"Please come down; before you hurt yourself," said the governess in more conciliatory tones. The little girl turned to face her, probably to glare at her because she was letting the side down.

By this time he had reached the highest point which could be reached without encountering branches which were too thin to safely bear his weight. He debated with himself whether he should reveal his identity or remain silent in the hope that they would go away. In the end, good manners prevailed and he shouted down to them that he was Roger Evesham.

"Why didn't you say so before," the little girl complained, loudly. "I think it is horrid of you to tease me in this way. At this, the governess nodded, although all he could see was the top of her head moving forward and back.

"Sorry," he hailed down, "I'm coming down, now," and suiting the action to the word, he began to descend. Unfortunately, when he was about eight feet from the ground, he missed his footing and fell flat on his back in the grass at their feet.

"Serves you right," said Amelia, haughtily, with a stamp of her foot.

He was too winded to speak and so he simply lay there with his eyes closed. His silence lasted so long that Amelia became agitated.

"Is he killed?" said Amelia in hushed tones to her governess.

"No dear, he is still breathing," she replied, in an even tone.

He opened his eyes to see them bending over him. In the same moment, Amelia gave out an audible gasp; she must have been relieved to see him open his eyes. She had her hands clasped together under her chin and her face was white. Despite her earlier crossness, she must feel real concern for him, after all; was his first thought. His second was that she was very pretty, albeit in a rather china-doll way.

He was still shaken, but attempted to struggle to his feet. When it was clear that he was having some difficulty, he was assisted by the governess. Amelia looked on, bewildered, as if he were a strange animal of some kind, or as if he had fallen out of a clear sky.

After he had dusted himself down, he introduced himself more formally with handshakes, after which they parted. He, to his side of the river, they, up the hill down which they had come. At one point, he looked up to see the little girl watching him. He waved to her and she waved back.

Suddenly, in the present day, the sound of the luncheon gong rang out and the reverie was brought to an end. He opened his eyes and images of the library intruded themselves upon his consciousness, once more.

One fragment of that memory remained, however: Amelia had told him, when they became better acquainted, later, that she had written of their very first encounter in her diary. She had never permitted him to read this journal during the time they were together, not even after they became engaged, although she had, from time to time, indicated that she was still an active diarist.

What she had written, in her round, childish hand, of that first meeting was in fact, as follows. "I met Roger Evesham today he lives on the neighbouring estate and so is a neighbour of ours. He is the son of a baronet and so is beneath me and my family. I met him when he fell out of a tree (it was my tree anyway not his) he didn't cry although he must have hurt himself. He is brave I suppose. I thought he was dead when he lay there on the ground because he was so very still. I was wrong. I'm quite glad he didn't die because he has a nice face. He isn't very tall but he is stocky. He is ten years old. I like him even though his position is less than mine. I hope we can become sort of friends because I have no-one of my own age to talk to. It is hard sometimes being a girl and I would rather talk to other girls. But if I see Roger again he will have to do instead."

FOUR

It was nine-thirty the next morning, Sunday, and the valet was putting the finishing touches to Roger's wing collar and tie pin just prior to his going to church. When Roger looked in the cheval glass he noted that his face wore a troubled expression.

He was unhappy because going to church on a Sunday had become something of an ordeal for him; it meant seeing Lady Amelia, her father and mother, and, worst of all, Charles.

Charles, of course, was not entitled to sit in the Hindthorpe family pew; not yet anyway, and Roger clung to the hope that that particular atrocity might never come to pass, but Charles was usually to be found skulking in one of the pews near the back of the church when he was in residence at the house he had taken in a neighbouring village; this event was surprisingly and happily, rare, due to some research work he was doing for a learned paper on pre-reformation churches, to be published by the university the following spring.

Roger, having made certain he was presentable, dismissed his valet and having taken up his carefully brushed silk top hat, left his dressing room and descended the stairs to the front vestibule of the house where, he could see through the glass-panelled doors, his carriage awaited him.

His mother was too sick that day to attend church, but she had been carried down to the little chapel in the east wing, earlier, and they had made their devotions there, together, as they always did when she was unwell; before Roger left for the village church.

It was a damp morning after heavy rain during the night;

but now it seemed that the attenuated sun of early October was trying to break through the grey sky in patches here and there.

As the carriage made its way down the long gravel drive it passed through several places where there was grimy standing water and this vexed Roger, who disliked arriving at the church in a mud-spattered carriage.

The carriage pulled up outside the church where several others stood already and Roger got down near the lych-gate. The rector was standing near to the entrance to the church greeting the worshippers. Roger nodded and smiled at him and exchanged a few words about the inclement weather.

As he entered his eyes strayed left and right, looking for Charles' elegant figure; he didn't seem to be there that Sunday and Roger relaxed a little. Even if he turned up now he wouldn't have to run the gauntlet of his presence and would be able to avoid him after the service.

He took his lonely seat about half-way down the Evesham family pew to the left of the aisle at the front and he knew without looking that the Hindthorpe family pew opposite would contain Lord and Lady Hindthorpe, Lady Amelia, and any guest or guests the family might have staying with them at that time. He did not as much as glance in their direction. The terrible situation was as difficult for them as for him and he fervently hoped that relations between the two families could be repaired one day.

The service ended and everybody stood up to leave the church, Roger had begun to think of the problem set him by the prime minister, just before the end of the last hymn and so he wasn't thinking about the Hindthorpes until his eyes met those of Amelia as she left her pew.

Something about her impassive face and unseeing eyes stabbed him to the heart in a way no dagger could have done. It was so great a shock to his system that he physically stumbled and would have fallen had not some of the trance worn off in time for him to steady himself with his hand on the back of the pew. He recovered his presence of mind sufficiently to take up a position facing the altar with a bowed head and closed eyes, as if in silent prayer instead of the turmoil he felt in reality, as the Hindthorpes moved past him and went down the aisle.

He stood there until there was silence and he knew he was alone, and then he picked up his hat and went out. He shook the rector's hand and mumbled something about it having been a good sermon, and then he quickly sought the sanctuary of his carriage. Luckily, the delay he had been forced to make before leaving the church meant that everyone had dispersed before he came out.

As the carriage made its way back to the house he wondered, not for the first time, if he might plead a temporary indisposition which would make it impossible to attend church services for a while.

What would his father have advised? He asked himself. As he knew already, his father would have told him that feigning illness to avoid something was tempting fate and that it would serve him right if a real illness supervened. He sighed and forced himself to observe the various shades of russet beginning to form in the leaves of the trees as the carriage went by them.

He dined with his mother that evening as he always did on a Sunday. She sat in a specially adapted chair which had been carried downstairs by two strong male kitchen servants.

It was a sombre meal, in the light of the flickering candles of the candelabras on the table, not just because of his sorrowful mood but because he became aware that his mother's failing appetite was more evident that evening than on the previous Sunday. He did not want to think about the possible implications of this.

After they had finished their meal and bade each other a

'good night' he went to the library to smoke some cigars and drink some fine brandy.

He toyed with a volume of Gibbon but found that the words danced on the page and he could not read them. In the event he drank more brandy than he intended, but it had the effect of calming his mind before he went upstairs.

As he undressed for bed, he more than once looked out of the diamond-leaded windows towards Hindthorpe Hall, two miles away across fields and forest, but there was nothing but blackness. He knew perfectly well that it was impossible to see Hindthorpe Hall from his bedroom window, or indeed from any window of Evesham Meads, even in broad daylight, but memories of looking out at night in that direction and deriving comfort from the fact that Amelia was out there somewhere, safely tucked up in bed, had compelled him to do so. Despite the circumstances of their estrangement, he still loved her and didn't want any misfortune to befall her. Her self-possessed attitude, he believed, was something of a masquerade; he had always felt instinctively that she needed his special protection. God only knew what kind of protection she would receive from Charles, he thought, shaking his head, sadly.

After deliberating this question for some little time he finally got into his four-poster and blew out the candle.

It was strange, he thought, before he went off to sleep, how big the bed seemed since the cancellation of their engagement. Before, it had always seemed exactly the right size, but then he had always been able to imagine her lying next to him, and had, so to speak, made room for her against the time when she would be there in reality.

He could remember the day that he officially announced his engagement as if it been yesterday, it was one of the proudest days of his life; perhaps it was actually the proudest.

He had of course asked her father for her hand some time

before and he had readily assented; it could hardly have come as a surprise to Lord Hindthorpe, because he and Amelia had been so very close for such a long time and there had never been any serious rivals.

Despite this, Roger was aware of the difference in rank which existed between the two men; a lord was superior to a baronet, but there were considerations which facilitated the match. For example, the Evesham title was older than that of Hindthorpe, also their estates were of a similar size, produced similar incomes and employed the same or a similar number of workers; if anything Roger's income was slightly higher than that of Lord Hindthorpe. Without these other factors, there was a distinct possibility that her father would not have accepted his suit.

The engagement had been announced at a summer hunt ball immediately after the meal and just before the commencement of the dancing, at the ballroom at Evesham Meads. The nobility and gentlefolk of two counties had been in attendance; a total of more than one hundred souls.

Roger, one of the masters of hounds and resplendent in the full regalia of swallowtail hunting pink, silk shirt and bow tie, black breeches, stockings and shoes, stood on the balcony overlooking the ballroom with a flushed and excited Amelia by his side.

He first called for silence and then made the announcement; this was followed by generous applause from the assembled company. Several young ladies hurried up the staircase to see the engagement ring, which featured a large diamond in a circlet of sapphires, and Amelia was more than happy to show it to them, amid a flurry of female embraces, kisses, and excited chatter and laughter. All the nearby men, young and old came up and shook Roger rather gravely by the hand, wishing them both well.

The handshaking and congratulations, paid to them both,

went on sporadically throughout the evening; somehow always taking them by surprise, because they kept thinking that everyone must have participated.

Roger even became convinced that he had shaken hands several times with some of the younger men; who must have been taking part in some kind of prearranged, good-natured conspiracy.

When he and Amelia came down the staircase to start the dance he felt as if he had drunk several magnums of champagne instead of the three glasses he had drunk that evening.

They stood facing each other, alone on the floor of the ballroom and at a signal from him the orchestra began to play a waltz. As they moved around the floor together, more and more couples joined them until the floor was crowded, and yet, it seemed to him that he and Amelia were the only couple there, so light-headed and intoxicated did he feel. He could tell by her radiance that she felt the same way; they were the happiest couple in England, in the world, in the universe; there had never been two happier people, ever, in the history of the world. Roger was mindful of the fact that he was being tautological in his reminiscences and was unapologetic for so being, because, nevertheless, the words did not adequately express the way he had felt, then.

A little later, he and Amelia slipped away to the gardens; they wanted to be alone, away from the hurly-burly of the ballroom which had become very hot and stuffy with some of the younger men beginning to get rather unruly.

They strolled in the moonlight along the paths which led to the fountains where it it was certain to be cool and refreshing. He dusted a nearby stone bench with his handkerchief and they sat and held hands; her bare shoulders and breasts above her décolletage were luminous in the pale light.

"You have made me the happiest of men," he declared.

"I am the happiest of women," she replied.

They embraced, and he kissed her for a long time, too long perhaps, for she gently broke away, with a little parting kiss and a sigh. After that, they sat holding hands and looking outwards at the fountains which made a peaceful plashing sound which he had scarcely noticed earlier. They seemed to be lost in their separate thoughts until a nearby owl screeched with surprising loudness, startling them back to each other once more.

"Are you cold?" he asked her, solicitously.

"I am a little," she replied. "I left my shawl in the house; I never thought I would need it."

"Would you like to borrow my jacket?" he asked.

"But then, dearest, you will soon be too cold," she replied.

"Perhaps, we should go back?" he said.

"Oh. I don't want to to that, just yet. I want to be with you in the moonlight, even if I freeze; I want to drink in this magical time."

He placed his hands on her shoulders, but they did not seem very chilled. He looked into her face and there was just enough light to see that she was smiling at him. He gently rubbed her shoulders to warm them and her smile faded a little. His action seemed to release some of the perfume she had been using that evening, because its scent became momentarily very strong and the headiness he had been feeling all evening increased and he momentarily felt an insane urge to plunge one of his hands down between her breasts.

Somehow, Amelia must have intuited this, because she suddenly seized his right hand and placed it, palm down, just below the nape of her neck. "I am yours, Roger; you know that. But we must be patient."

It was this contrast between the way Amelia gently rejected him, with its overtones of high moral standards, compared with her almost headlong dash into bed with Charles, which really

38

cut him to the quick; sometimes the pain of it was almost unbearable. Why had she found the love thing with him so very unattractive? What attributes in that regard did Charles possess that he did not?

FIVE

One morning, in late July, about a month after she had broken off her engagement to Roger, Lady Amelia awakened in the four-poster bed and looked around the bedroom of the house Charles had taken for the summer. She saw with approval that the sun was shining outside, showing itself through a crack in the curtains; she could hear the birds singing in the trees outside the window.

The silver carriage clock on her bedside table showed that it was half-past seven and yet she felt that she had had enough sleep. A faint susurration near her head reminded her that Charles lay in the bed next to her. Raising her head a little she could see that his arm, which had been wounded in the duel and which still gave him some pain, was lying outside the covers.

The poor lamb sometimes lay upon it in his sleep and then the gentle sound of his breathing changed to groans and she would gently help him onto his back or his other side. Sometimes, if he was only partially awake, he would kiss her as a reward for this service. At other times, he would awaken fully, fold her into his arms, and take her passionately. This was a passion which she wholeheartedly shared. She felt at times that she could never have enough of it and would ultimately die without being utterly sated.

Afterwards, as she drifted off to sleep, she would feel that she was the luckiest woman alive; except for the deep disapproval of her parents and all her other relatives concerning the life she was now living; but this was a matter of only the slightest moment to her, so intoxicated was she by the freedom from convention she experienced.

Those of her relatives whose ears were too tender to be told of the great scandal which surrounded her were simply kept away from her, whenever she visited her ancestral home; as if her presence would taint them in some way and lead them, also, into a life of depravity and sin.

She lay naked in the warm bedclothes and luxuriated in the time before getting up for the day. The trouble with a life of depravity and sin, she knew, was that she enjoyed every minute and every second of every day. Charles was a man who seemed to have powerful urges, where a woman was concerned, and he took her at least three times every day and sometimes more. She couldn't imagine her stiff and pompous erstwhile fiancé doing that, or anything like it. He didn't know what physical love could be like, she was certain, or so-called spiritual love, either.

Yesterday had been one of those days when Charles had needed her more than usual and they had also coupled three times during the night. She felt a soreness in her loins, her body felt a bit battered and she knew she had some bruises. But these small injuries sustained in the act of love were of no consequence, she did not care if he hurt her a little; the only bodily sensation that mattered was the intense pleasure she felt every time they had congress.

He had once kissed her so fiercely during one particularly passionate moment that he had bruised her lips and she had had to chide him a little; but only because they had to think of the servants; they would see the bruising, because it could not be properly concealed, and think he was abusing her in some way.

He had been so very sorry about it and had promised to try and be more careful of her face and any part of her person which might be seen during the day; her neck, her arms and the upper part of her breasts, for example, which she liked to show off by wearing dresses with low décolletage in the evenings. But he

41

had not been able to be certain that he could or would, because he enjoyed her body so much that he tended to forget such niceties. She had adored him the more for this confession; it was so in tune with the way she herself felt during their couplings.

She felt him stirring and at once felt the excitement she always felt when they were in bed together, unfettered by any clothing. Would he take her again this morning or would he be spent by the exertions of the night?

He turned his head and his lazuli eyes were open. He smiled at her in that way of his which made every cell in her body cry out for his embrace.

He held his arms open for her, she came to him and they shared the first kiss of the day.

"I love you, my darling," he said afterwards, in his wonderful French accent, which, when combined with the situation they were in, made her think of him as love personified; both physical and spiritual.

"And I love you, my darling," she affirmed; her body beginning to tremble as his hands sought and cupped her firm and generous breasts.

They kissed once again, this time firmly and lingeringly, so that she could feel her blood begin to tingle, then they made love vivace, by unspoken mutual consent, so that their passion was quickly spent.

Afterwards, Amelia kissed him on the lips in a valedictory way, got out of the bed, partially drew the curtains, and stood in front of the open window so that the air could dry her perspiration and cool her naked body.

"Be careful, my sweet," said Charles who had pulled himself up into a sitting position, the better to admire her. "You don't want someone to see you in state of undress and think you are a bigger whore than they do already."

Amelia turned towards him and smiled at him; that she was supposed to be a whore or trollop was a private joke between them. "Don't worry, dearest one, no one can see me at this window without a telescope; the open field outside provides no possible place of concealment anywhere near."

He smiled wickedly. "How do you know that somebody has not gone to the trouble and expense of obtaining such an optical aid?"

He was teasing her, she knew, and she loved him for it. Nevertheless, she quickly moved away from the window in mock alarm and put on a dressing gown preparatory to ringing down for the upstairs maidservant; so that baths for Charles and herself could be drawn in their adjacent bathrooms.

She sat on a low stool in front of her dressing table and began combing the tangles out of her hair; while Charles, whom she could see in the mirror, lit a cigar and watched her with a fond expression. As he sat there cross-legged naked on the bed; his olive skin showed that he was of European blood.

Later, after they had bathed, they had their breakfast outside on the veranda, for it was a warm day, using two folding card tables set together for their board.

Things were still a bit rudimentary at Charles' house, reflected Amelia, as she ate her breakfast, but he had promised her better things when they went to France in the late autumn; academic and business interests would keep him in England until then; he was researching pre-reformation churches for a paper to be presented to the university before they left England. Then they would have a big wedding in Paris and after that he was going to petition the French government for the return of his chateau and estate.

"What do you want to do today, darling?" he asked, smiling at her. He had trimmed and waxed his moustache after his bath, so that it and he looked particularly fine and handsome.

Amelia had not given this any mind, she was just very happy to be with the man she loved. As she thought this, a curious slight pang of distress went through her heart. After a pause, she realised that this had to do with her former feelings for Roger; this resurgence surprised her, but it passed as quickly as it arrived and afterwards she became aware that Charles was looking quizzically at her, waiting for an answer.

"Oh I don't know," she said. "Perhaps, I might go sketching down by the river, I was there yesterday and it was so lovely that I felt I must make a few pencil sketches and perhaps, on another day, begin something in watercolour or oils. And you?"

"I thought I would go for a walk around the boundaries of the property to see that everything, fences and so on, are in good order. Perhaps, I could meet you at the river at about midday, when we could have a picnic luncheon?"

"That would be very nice; what a good idea."

"Do you want me to carry the sketching materials down there, for you?"

Amelia smiled at his thoughtfulness. "No Charles, I am only going to take the camp stool, a block, some pencils and an eraser; hardly any weight to carry."

After they finished breakfast, they kissed and each went to their dressing rooms to change out of the dressing gowns they both still wore. Amelia decided to wear a white summer dress, decorated with pastel flowers, and a straw bonnet to keep the sun from her eyes.

Charles, after looking through his wardrobes, decided on a pale-grey suit, without the waistcoat, a white, collarless shirt and a panama. He could not decide whether to wear a cravat or not, and in the end simply wore his shirt with the top button open.

He went to the window which afforded a view of the distant river and in the middle distance could see Amelia wending her way down the footpath which led there. She carried a basket and had a light, folding, camp stool with a canvas seat, which he had bought for her at the Army and Navy stores, tucked under one arm; so that she could sit with the sketch block on her knees. How pretty and elegant she looked, he thought with some regret.

Charles drank a last cup of cold coffee, which he had brought up from the veranda before Mary the cook's assistant could clear away the breakfast dishes, then he went downstairs, leaving the cup and saucer carelessly on the hallstand. He selected a Malacca cane from the elephant's foot near the inside of the front door and went out into the sunshine.

Amelia had begun sketching using a selection of pencils of varying hardness and shade from George Rowney and Co. She was a fairly good artist, but she knew she was no Monet, an artist whose style she admired and attempted to copy when she painted in oils. After a time she had to stop and sharpen the pencils with a folding pocket knife. The knife slipped and cut the little finger of her left hand. It was only a slight cut and she inserted the finger into her mouth, taking it out from time to time to see if it had stopped bleeding. When the flow of blood was almost staunched she tied a corner of her handkerchief around it; then went back to work on her sketch. To her annoyance, a few drops of blood had fallen in a little group on the foreground of the landscape she had begun drawing and had dried there. She looked at them for a few minutes and then decided to turn them into poppies even though it was the wrong time of the year for those. With a few deft strokes here and there, she turned the three drops of blood into three poppies whose flowers were red but whose stems and leaves were only outlined in pencil.

Charles had deliberately taken a route which led in the opposite direction to that taken by Amelia; he needed time to think and the best place to think, he had found, was when he

45

was out for a walk in the country, alone.

He had seen and recruited most of the people and had arranged for most of the supplies to be delivered to the abandoned Hall. He would have to go down there in a few days to coordinate the project. He was often away and he and Amelia had had words on the subject, but he had made her believe that his times away were for their mutual benefit and that things would be different when they got to France. He could not tell her the truth about his work, of course, she was an Englishwoman through and through. He smiled ruefully at this.

Luckily, she was expendable in the overall scheme of things, but at the moment she provided valuable cover for his activities in England; not to mention a certain amount of comfort and happiness when he was at home.

Charles had reached a wall which he knew he had climb over if he did not want to walk more than a mile out of his way. He scrambled to find a suitable foothold, and then winced at the pain in his shoulder as he heaved himself up to the top, prior to jumping down into the meadow on the other side. The wound, although completely healed, still gave him sharp twinges at certain times.

Charles stood at the edge of the field and looked across to the hedge on the other side where a small herd of dairy cows were grazing. He took out his watch and saw it was almost eleven. He patted his pockets to reassure himself that he remembered to bring his cigar case and vestas and then he set off across the meadow on a diagonal route which would bring him to a gate which opened onto the lane which ran down one side of the property.

He would walk down the lane, which also went around the front lawns of the house and continue on until he had completed his inspection of the bounds; then he would fetch the makings of a picnic lunch from the kitchens and carry them down to where Amelia was sketching.

He reached the gate and stood leaning against it smoking a cigar, so far he had not seen a soul, but now a milk cart with four churns on it came slowly up the lane, driven by a very old man who delivered milk to various houses in the district, including his. He waved his whip at Charles in greeting as he passed. From the booming sounds which came from the churns as the cart went over irregularities in the surface in the lane, Charles guessed that they were empty, that he had finished his round and was probably going back to the dairy in the nearby village for a well-earned lunch.

Charles reached the stone bridge under which a river flowed; this was the same river on whose banks Amelia now sat sketching, unless she had tired of it and gone indoors. He smiled at how unlikely this was; Amelia was such a determined girl, she seldom gave up on anything half-way through.

Looking upriver, Charles thought he could discern a dot of white in the middle distance. As he watched, the dot moved a little and then went back to its original position. Almost certainly, the dot was Amelia trying out different viewpoints and perspectives.

Since the river formed the boundary of the lower part of the property there was no point in going further up the lane and Charles retraced his steps to the beginning of the carriage drive which led to the house. When he reached the front door he looked at his watch, it was ten past twelve. The picnic luncheon would be a little late, he reflected, as he headed for the kitchens to collect the picnic hamper he had ordered earlier. He had intended to change his shirt before he met Amelia; he had no time for that now, she would be displeased with him if he was any later than he already was.

Amelia sat on the little stool, near the edge of the river, the sketch block on her knees and a pencil in her hand, but there was no movement; it was as if she had been frozen in that position.

She was lost in her thoughts and she didn't want to be; she tried very hard not to dwell too much on any aspect of her life with Charles; doing so caused her, sooner or later, to become fearful about their future together.

Charles was very distant to her, sometimes, and it upset her so; she wanted him to think only of her and he so obviously did not. She had even fallen to wondering if he had another woman. There was absolutely no evidence that that was the case.

He was wrestling with some mighty problem or problems, she knew, and he sometimes had male friends to stay who were polite to her in a very detached manner. The visitor, or visitors, for there was sometimes more than one, always went with Charles to his study after dinner, where they locked themselves in and talked in low voices, leaving her alone for hours. Sometimes, he didn't come to bed until she had been asleep half the night. It had got to the point where her heart sank whenever she heard that they were to entertain yet another of his friends.

Another odd thing was that these people, for the most part, were not gentlemen, let alone aristocracy. Although he sometimes introduced them as such, they were clearly not friends from his Oxford days. It was a puzzle, as was the fact that he often hid whatever papers he was working with whenever she came to the study to ask him about anything, when he was alone, that is; he never permitted her to interrupt him when he had company with him.

Charles did seem to love her, as much as she loved him, but it was the difference in kind not in degree which worried her at times like this when she became introspective. Although fearful of the consequences of bringing a bastard child into the world, she wished with all her heart that she was pregnant. So far, this had not happened, and she could not understand why, because she gave herself to him so utterly, with all her heart and soul, with something approaching desperation every time they had congress, and yet each month the show of menses mocked her hopes.

Perhaps he was at fault in some way, perhaps he could not have children. She knew perfectly well that he had had liaisons with many women, before they met, because he made no secret of the fact. On the other hand, he had always been sensitive to her feelings when he had outlined his experiences with these other women. He had told her that he needed to confess these things to her, that he felt in some way dishonoured by them and that he never wanted anyone else to have the opportunity to reveal an affair of his to her which might cause their wonderful relationship to be sundered to pieces at some point in the future.

This would become even more important, he said, when they went to live in Paris and his friends and relatives came to their house to pay their respects. He was particularly anxious that there not be any possibility of any embarrassment for her, real or imagined, at that crucial time.

She had understood all this and loved him the more for it. Also, at that time, when he wanted to make a clean breast of his previous life, she had asked him something which she had feared above all else: whether or not he had ever been married before. He had sworn that he had not.

This left one question which she had not had the courage to ask him at that time, or since, and it was one to which she had become more and more determined to have an answer, because of the light it could throw upon her childless state: had any of these liaisons ever produced a child?

She heard a slight sound and looked up to see the approach of Charles bearing a picnic hamper, a blanket and a folding stool similar to her own. In the same instant she discovered to her surprise that she was crying. She hastily wiped away the tears with her tiny handkerchief and managed to compose herself sufficiently to smile when he got to within a few yards of her; however, his answering smile was quickly replaced by a concerned expression when he got close enough to see her face clearly.

"Hello!" he said, after he had placed his burdens on a dry part of the riverbank. "You look as if you have been crying. Is the sketching going badly?"

"It has nothing to do with the sketching, Charles. I have reached a decision, that is all." She looked at him with something like defiance.

Charles looked distinctly uneasy. "What is it, my dearest? I hope you don't regret your decision to throw Roger over, for me?"

"Of course not, Charles!" she replied vehemently, rising, with her sketch block in her hand and moving to his side, where she kissed him on the cheek. "Nothing could be further from my mind," she went on.

Charles beamed with relief, but then his face became concerned, once more. "But there is something which troubles you."

"Yes, Charles; but it is not as serious as that."

"What then?"

"I so want to have a child by you, Charles, and nothing seems to have happened, so far, although we live as man and wife."

"Is that all?" he said, smiling. "It's still very early days, my love. Sometimes, it takes a while for a woman's body to adjust."

This was the cue she had been hoping for. "Have you ever had a child by any of your women, Charles?" she blurted, before her thoughts got in the way of her asking.

Charles was a bit taken aback, but he smiled indulgently. "That's a question I never expected from you, an aristocrat's daughter. Surely, that would come under the rubric of 'things not spoken of in decent society'."

"I know, Charles. I know," said Amelia with a sob in her voice. "It's just that I have to know whether you can have children, because if not, then it must be me. I have been so worried and distressed about this question."

"Then I have to tell you that I have two children, a boy and a girl, by two different women and that I have made provision for all concerned. I am sorry to give you the answer that will distress you most, in the light of what you said about your fear of being barren. But I know that not being open and honest about this matter would only cause it to prey on your mind."

Amelia began to sob very quietly, in earnest, Charles held her tightly to him, and for a time they stood there in a silence broken only by the faint rushing sound of the river and occasional birdsong.

"It is possible that the trouble lies in the irregularity of our relationship," said Charles a little later, when her sobs had almost ceased. "When I lived in France, I heard about such things from a doctor who was a good friend of mine."

"I don't know what you mean, Charles," said Amelia, in a perplexed tone.

Charles led her to her camp stool and gently helped her to sit there, and then he fetched his, opened it, and sat facing her at a distance of a few feet. He held out his hand to her and she clasped it and looked at him expectantly.

"It is just that sometimes the mind of the woman is apparently willing, but the body rebels," said Charles, solemnly.

"I don't know what you mean by 'apparently willing'," said Amelia.

"It may seem impossible, but sometimes in a woman the body and the mind appear to be in agreement with one another, but the truth is that her body knows there exists a part of her mind which is deeply unhappy about the circumstances of the relationship she has entered into and this interferes with the chemistry, for want of a better word, of normal conception."

Amelia shook her head. "I cannot believe you Charles, what you say is too fantastic."

"I assure you, once again, my dearest Amelia, I have heard of such things. A woman of my acquaintance, for instance, who gave herself desperately to the man she hoped to marry; but he was a blackguard who used women for his pleasure, with no intention of ever doing the right thing by them. She never conceived with him, but when he deserted her, as everyone knew he would, she conceived almost immediately when she fell in love with, and subsequently married, a good and decent man."

She began to stare at him in horror and suddenly released his hand. "Are you saying that you are an unsuitable man for me? That you, too, are a species of blackguard?"

"No, of course I am not saying that. What I am saying is that some part of your mind is unhappy about your situation with me. Probably because we are not yet married." Charles had known that she would turn his explanation against him in the way she had, but had nevertheless felt compelled to speak to her of it; he had not wanted her to blame herself for her childless state.

Amelia fell silent for some time as she considered his revelation, then at last she spoke. "It is true, Charles, that a part of me is unhappy about not being married to you, but I still don't think it sufficient reason for my barrenness." She looked at him sadly and a little resentfully.

Charles took her hand once more and smiled kindly at her. At times like this he could be very kind, she thought. "But that is my whole point, *mon petite choux*; the situation doesn't depend upon what you consciously think."

"But, perhaps we will never be all right and I will never have a child by you," said Amelia, again with a sob in her voice.

52

"Everything will be all right between us when we are married and are living in Paris as man and wife."

"You really think so?" she said, eagerly, gazing intently into his eyes.

"Of course, sweet love of my life, I know so."

She rose suddenly and clasped him to her tightly; knocking over her camp stool in the process. He pulled her onto his lap and there was a loud creaking sound as his stool complained at the extra weight it had to bear. They both laughed as she quickly got up. Then, righting her stool, she sat opposite him once more and took his hand.

"That's better," he said, relieved at her laughter. "Now perhaps we can have our lunch with a better face on everything."

"Oh, how I love you, Charles," she said gazing adoringly at him.

"How I love you too," he returned, gazing adoringly at her.

They ate their lunch in an atmosphere of the most perfect contentment.

SIX

A few days passed and Roger had received a communication that morning from the office of the prime minister. It concerned the gunpowder which had been confiscated from the cottage of the smuggler.

Apparently, since his interview with Gladstone, the three unmarked barrels of powder had been taken to the arsenal at Woolwich for analysis, so that an attempt could be made to determine the country of origin; because different countries used slightly different compositions of the three ingredients, as well as different charcoals; which could, after the nitre and sulphur had been removed using the appropriate solvents, be identified under the microscope.

It was the opinion of the experts at Woolwich that the powder had been manufactured in the powder mills at Liège, Belgium and was the finest quality, fine-grained sporting powder.

Roger took the letter to his study and placed it in the locked drawer where he now kept the police report, the poetry book and the papers which had contained the coded messages; together with his worked solutions.

He had carefully checked the personal columns of *The Evening news* every day since he had found the coded messages featured therein, but no new messages had appeared; so he turned his attention, once more, to the drawing, under the last poem in the poetry book, of the orange horseshoe with twelve red nail-holes. It might mean something, he reasoned, or it might have no significance, but, either way, he would do his very best to find a reference to it in his library, or failing that, in the reading room of the British Museum for which he had a great love and respect; he had a reader's ticket, as had his father before him, and was familiar with the protocol of the reading room.

The library at Evesham Meads was an unusual one because of his father's interest in a large number of disparate subjects. His father had travelled extensively as a young man, all over the world, but especially in the countries of Europe and added all kinds of books to an already extensive collection.

Roger, when a boy, had often had lengthy discussions with his father about the knowledge he had acquired, both in terms of the printed word and as a result of his adventures abroad. His father had, luckily, recorded most if not all these in the form of travel journals, together with some beautiful illustrations executed by him; for, among his many accomplishments, he had been an artist of some note. Roger intended to consult these journals as part of his library search.

Although he had never said so in as many words, Roger had known, even as a boy, that his father had been searching for something during his forays abroad. Later, on his deathbed, he had confirmed this belief of his son, because he had told him that he had indeed been engaged on such a search, but had never been able to find the thing he sought, or even define it, saying only that if he ever had encountered it he would at once have recognised it, whatever it was.

Shaking his head over the sadness of this, Roger began the lengthy task of trying to find a reference to a horseshoe of the kind depicted; in words or by way of an illustration, or ideally, both.

There were thousands of books in the library, but he began with the books of reference, such as encyclopaedias and dictionaries.

After more than seven hours of intensive searching, pausing only to take a hurried lunch of sandwiches and coffee, he was forced to take a break; all that knowledge was making his brain sing like a kettle.

He pulled an armchair into a better position before the fireplace; the fire was burning now that the maids once again had access, and lit a cigar from it using a spill kept with some others in a German beer stein on the mantelpiece.

He felt dispirited by this total lack of any success and began to realise that he was unlikely to come across the information he desperately needed, using only the comparatively meagre resources of his library. He would have to go up to town and seek help at the British Museum library. Perhaps, he could combine the trip to town with the handing in of his report to the prime minister. He could only do that if he was granted a proper appointment.

He went to the writing desk and dashed off a quick letter to Number Ten, then rang for the butler and gave it to him to post. After he finished his cigar he went back to the task in hand.

At six he gave it up for the day, he would have to wash and dress for dinner soon and, despite the sandwiches, he was famished. The activity of his brain had burned up all his blood sugar, he surmised.

After dinner, since the weather was clement, he decided to go for a brisk walk to the folly, high on the hill behind the house, before bedtime. This folly, which had been built by his grandfather, was an approximation in miniature of the Acropolis in Athens.

It was a chilly evening, so he wore his ulster, scarf and tweed hat. He made sure that he had some vestas and his cigar case before he set off. It was a stiff climb but he usually felt better for it and this evening was no exception.

The folly had a roof but was otherwise open to the elements via the pillars which supported it. He sat on one of the stone benches, the one which afforded a view of the way he had come and the house, and lit a cigar.

The trouble with the folly was that it had been one of his and Amelia's favourite trysting places, but since almost every landmark on his six-thousand two hundred and fifty acres had been used at one time or another for that purpose, he had, some time ago, realised that he could hardly avoid these places altogether; simply because of their unhappy associations.

It was not very long before those associations prompted him to take up the story, once again, just after the tree-climbing incident.

He and Amelia had begun a tentative, at first, friendship. This was partly because, in their early days, her governess invariably accompanied her at all times. But, when this woman fell ill with influenza, they were allowed to spend a limited amount of time together, provided they stayed within sight and sound of Amelia's house. Gradually, these rules were relaxed, and even after the governess recovered they were allowed to play and roam further and further from civilisation, so to speak, without supervision.

Released from her governess and her disapproving gaze, Amelia had soon shown signs of being headstrong and tomboyish. Though hampered by her long skirts and petticoats, she could run surprisingly quickly and also insisted on climbing trees, especially the tree where they had first met. Although she was not really in his charge, he knew that he would get into hot water very quickly if she were ever hurt or injured while in his company and this gave him cause for concern, especially since she often teased him with the consequences of her more boisterous actions.

"If I hurt myself, you will get the blame," she would jeer from one precarious vantage point or another.

"Yes. I know," he would reply with resignation.

This conversation took place with such monotonous regularity that he could have made the responses in his sleep. In the end, a stratagem occurred to him.

"You do enjoy playing with me, don't you?" he enquired of her one day when they were recovering their breath on the summit of a cliff after some hair-raising rock climbing.

"Yes, of course I do," she said, smiling. She had a very warm and sunny smile, it was one of the many reasons he enjoyed being with her.

"But you know what they will do if you are hurt and blame me?" he said. Both children had fallen into the habit of referring to the grown-ups, of both families, and in general, as 'they'.

"No. What will they do?"

"They will not allow us to play together, ever again." He knew this to be true. In fact, it was nothing short of miraculous that this had not yet happened. There had been a few occasions when she had torn her clothes or got her feet wet, or suffered some other small misadventure. On these occasions, he had held his breath, on parting from her for the day, and had resigned himself to never seeing her again, or perhaps not for years; happily, his fears so far had proved to be groundless.

She sat silently beside him for a minute or so, digesting his pronouncement, then she spoke. "I will make a bargain with you," she said, her face grave, "if I suffer any injury to my person or clothing, I will tell them that it happened after I left your company. I promise never to give you away." She looked earnestly at him and he saw for the first time that their time together meant as much to her as it did him.

He held out his hand to show that he approved of her plan and she held out her hand, likewise. But they did not shake hands; instead, she presented her palm to him, with her fingers held straight up. He copied her and they pressed their palms together as hard as they could for a few seconds. This solemn act having been completed, their frowns of concentration vanished and they smiled happily at one another.

"I shall never give you away," she said.

"I shall never give you away," he repeated.

After that, they were closer than ever before, because he no longer had to think about the consequences when he or she suggested some new game or adventure and this lifted his spirits in a way which was infectious. It did not mean that they could be reckless, of course, but it gave them a greater leeway.

One of the most agreeable things about not being supervised by an adult was that they could go riding together, although both families issued dire warnings against riding at anything greater than a canter and forbade all and any kinds of jumps.

Still, it was very nice and aristocratic to go calling for her on his favourite chestnut stallion, when the weather was clement, with the gloss on his top hat and boots gleaming in the sun and all his clothes similarly immaculate. Then setting out together, Amelia on her favourite grey mare dressed in all her finery.

They made a handsome mounted couple and this was confirmed by the admiring glances they drew from all but the most surly estate workers as they passed. He and Amelia would nod and smile at them in concert and sometimes he would raise his hat if the personage warranted it.

They would ride side by side at a trotting pace, deep in conversation, and the distances they covered during those times never ceased to amaze him. The afternoons simply flew by and, depending on the season, it often began to get dark before they realised they had better wend their way home again.

Later, after they had ridden point-to-point a number of times and had otherwise displayed their skill and shown that they were strong, sensible riders, the rules were relaxed and they were allowed gallops and jumps.

On one especially memorable autumn day, soon after riding at speed was permitted, they had ridden in a leisurely way out to a grove of chestnut trees and he had managed, by standing up in the stirrups, to gather quantities of the prickly green bundles which had been missed by, or had been out of reach of, other gatherers.

So engrossed were they by this absorbing and happy task that the sun had dipped down almost to the horizon before they realised it was time to return home. They stowed the chestnut clusters in a saddle bag which had been brought by him for that purpose and set off.

At first they trotted, then they cantered, and finally as the dying sun disappeared behind some distant hills, they galloped furiously through fields where, here and there, were some mature oaks. They managed to avoid the lower branches of these and soon they reached the grassy chase which led straight down to her home.

They could just make out, in the fading light, Hindthorpe Hall, which stood at the far end of the chase, and they galloped neck and neck down it. It was not a race; it was simply two young people caught up in the exhilaration of the moment.

Roger quickly removed his top hat and held it tightly in one hand, because it would otherwise have been swept off his head in the first seconds of their furious ride.

The reached the stable yard at Hindthorpe Hall with the horses panting great clouds of vapour into the now-chilly air and with their flanks smoking, similarly. They got down at the mounting-blocks and the horses were covered with blankets and led away to warmth and shelter by stable lads.

He and Amelia repaired to her old nursery which she now used for her occasional hobby of embroidery and other forms of decorative sewing and weaving. Here, having doffed their outdoor wear, they sat on the floor before a small fire in order to remove the chestnuts from their cases. They worked over an old newspaper to keep the husks and debris from the carpet and used a stout paper bag to store the chestnuts; gleaming like cherished and polished wooden carvings.

After a few attempts to open the husks with their sharp spines, and pricking her delicate fingers painfully in the process, Amelia gave it up as a bad job and Roger was delegated by mutual consent to undertake this part of the proceedings, while Amelia gingerly took up and threw the empty husks into the fire, where they crackled and whistled in a peculiar manner as they burned.

At length, they had a bag containing about two dozen or so chestnuts which they now decided to roast after dinner, to which Roger had a standing invitation whenever he was a visitor at the Hall, on the bars of the much larger dining room fire.

In the event, while they were roasting, with Roger and Amelia sitting on a nearby rug looking on expectantly and Lord and Lady Hindthorpe indulgently, one of the chestnuts which had not been scored deeply enough or perhaps not at all, exploded with a sharp report, startling the old butler who was just bringing in the after-dinner sherry. Roger and Amelia could not help laughing and even the Lord and Lady permitted themselves discreet smiles.

Roger came out of this reverie with a smile which quickly vanished with a slight shudder as he contrasted the childish pact which had triggered this happy recollection with the modern-day reality of their ruined relationship. Still, he thought, as he stood and began to walk back to the house, throwing away the long-cold stub of his cigar en route, one's childish intentions and desires are hardly ever engraved in stone.

Did he love her, even then? He was unable to conjure up the way he felt at the time, but he believed that what he had felt for her was the innocent love which unrelated boys and girls felt before they reached puberty. That explosion of adulthood could either sunder or cement such a relationship. He had believed theirs had been cemented, until this terrible year. He gave a harsh laugh which he hastily turned into a clearing of the throat, in case someone was within earshot, and lit another cigar, which was still burning when he reached the house.

He sat before the fire in the library, with a glass of his favourite brandy warming and refluxing in his hand, gazing around gloomily at the acres of print which surrounded him. The answer to the question of the horseshoe design seemed now even less likely to lie within one or other of those volumes.

SEVEN

The following afternoon, after he had completed his estate work and taken luncheon, Roger was in his study putting the finishing touches to his interim report for the prime minister when he heard the discreet knock of Thompson, his butler. "Come," he said, loudly, and the butler entered bearing some letters on a silver salver. The mid-afternoon post had evidently just been delivered.

"Thank you," said Roger, taking the letters. The butler hesitated slightly, in case there were any further instructions; when he realised there were none, he bowed and quietly departed.

Roger examined the three letters, two related to estate business and were addressed in familiar hands; he and his estate manager would deal with them, together with the morning post, after breakfast on the morrow.

The third, however, was addressed in an unfamiliar hand and was postmarked Stepney at 10 p.m. the previous evening. He frowned; he had no correspondent who resided in that part of London, or anywhere near it. The white envelope was of medium quality and the address had been written in small upper-case letters, using ordinary black ink.

He opened the envelope and a folded half-sheet of matching notepaper fell out onto his desk.

8th October 1884

I know what work you are engaged upon (it read). If you

come to 12 Black Dog Lane, Stepney, at 9 o'clock p.m. on the 15th October you will learn something which will help you move forward. Come alone and knock twice.

A Friend.

The fifteenth of October was next Wednesday, six days hence, that was good, he would need a few days to prepare something in his workshop before then; it might be a trap and he was not going to take any chances.

He found that he could not go on with his report, for the time being, and put it away in its drawer. Instead, he found all his thoughts focused on the strange missive which he found himself reading over and over again. There was no salutation and the words were written in the same style as the address, using the same ink. There were no discernible watermarks, either in the envelope or in the letter, itself.

He leaned back in his chair and confessed himself baffled by this turn of events. First of all, who could this mysterious stranger be? How could anyone possibly know about the highly secret work he was engaged upon? Let alone someone who lived in an out-of-the way place like Stepney.

He would, of course, keep the appointment, but he would not tell anyone about it, not even the prime minister; in case it turned out to be an elaborate hoax.

Another idea occurred to him: the whole charade might be designed as a catch-all, to find out if he was engaged in some covert work or other. In that case, whoever had written the letter would know, if he kept the appointment, that something of the sort was occupying him. They would not discover what it was because he intended to take his revolver and shoot his way out of any situation which threatened to endanger his life or trap him into giving out any information.

Also, he intended to take along a certain little device which he had already designed and made in his head, and which he would soon make in reality, to add a tiny extra dimension to his safety on the evening in question. All-in-all he felt completely confident that he could accomplish his mission, alone, as specified in the letter.

Some small part of him felt that he should contact the police and let them handle the situation, but he immediately dismissed this idea; he would have a lot of explaining to do and those very explanations might compromise his work for the prime minister. The less people in the know about his work, the better. Besides, it was implicit in his original acceptance of Gladstone's assignment that he was on his own, no matter what might come.

Abruptly, he rose from his chair and, having locked the letter away, in the same drawer as the report, poetry book, and other documents relating to the case, he took the key of his workshop from another drawer and went upstairs.

The workshop had its origins in his boyhood, when he had begun to build model yachts to sail on one of the many ponds of the estate and, later, the Long Lake. It had come into existence because his nurse had complained long and loud to his father about wood shavings and spilled glue and varnish in the nursery, not to mention the awful smell which arose from the melted glue in the water-jacketed gluepot after he had taken it off the fire for use. In the end, his father, who had wanted to indulge his creative bent, had made a disused dressing room available to him, and had arranged for a bench and some shelves to be installed.

He had spent many happy hours ensconced in this room absorbed in hobbies which had included metalwork, he remembered, as he opened the door and it was this latter that he intended to concentrate on, now.

The room was very dusty and cobwebby, he couldn't

remember when he had been in here, last, but it must be something like ten years. All the tools were still intact and although a little rusty, still fit for purpose.

He would have to instruct the butler to instruct the housekeeper to ensure the place was given a thorough clean, the next day, before he could do any serious work, he realised. For now, he satisfied himself he had sufficient materials for his purpose. He then left the little room, locking the door after him. He would give the butler the instructions for the housekeeper a little later on, together with the key.

Next he went to the gunroom to select a suitable revolver. No-one but he ever came into this room with its glass-fronted gun racks filled with sporting guns, most were modern hammerless guns by Greener and Purdey, some were from the early part of the century and beyond; the muzzle-loading, double-barrelled flint and percussion guns which had belonged to his forefathers, some bearing the famous names of Egg, Nock, Manton and Westley-Richards. There were a few rifles, including rook rifles, and a couple of four-bore elephant guns.

There were also several glass-topped display cases containing the family collection of small-arms. One held a number of pairs of cased flintlock and percussion duelling pistols. Seeing these, last, brought back painful memories.

Also in the display cases were some curiosities such as percussion pepperboxes, all-steel highland pistols with ram's horn and heart-shaped butts, a Forsyth scent-bottle, a few Italian daggs, a duck's foot, a Le Mat and a few original Deringers and some Derringer copies by various manufacturers.

He turned to the display case which contained several modern revolvers and selected his favourite, a Webley Bulldog .38. This rather ungainly firearm had a comforting heaviness when carried in a greatcoat pocket.

So far, he had only ever used it for target shooting at the old archery butts on the estate, where he had become reasonably proficient in its use at twenty-five yards. In case he had become rusty, since then, he intended to practise there once or twice more before he went to Stepney.

That evening, after dinner, he fell to thinking about a person he had hitherto found it impossible to consider without feeling physically ill - Count Charles de Braquelin; it was seeing the duelling pistols, earlier, which had brought this on, he knew.

Whether it was because enough time had elapsed or whether the forthcoming errand with its overtones of danger had made him more devil-may-care, he found that he could hold images of him without too much pain. It was true that the man had formed the stuff of many of his nightmares until fairly recently, and he now began to consider the question of whether he had been too harsh in his judgement of him.

No. On the whole, he did not think he had been too hasty in forming the opinion which he now had. Even now, he would not be able to discuss him in all-male company without breaking out into a string of concatenated expletives. He sighed, this really would not do; he was a great believer in the ability of anger to corrosively destroy the person who bore it, especially anger of the magnitude he felt. He did not want to be destroyed in this way and so it seemed that he had to try and make sense of what was, on the face of it, incomprehensible.

He began by reviewing their first meeting, soon after he had gone up to Oxford three years ago; almost to the day.

He was still aching from a particularly poignant leave-taking, at the small local station, of his fiancée just before his train left for the university town. He stood in the carriage with the window fully down holding both of Amelia's hands while the tears ran unashamedly down her face and to a lesser extent his.

"It's only for seven weeks, my dearest," he said, his voice thick with the emotion which had been generated between them. Up until then, he had not realised how much he would miss her, nor, evidently, how much she would miss him.

"Couldn't you come home at weekends, sometimes?" she said with a hint of desperation in her voice.

"We have been through all that, dearest one" he replied. "It would be much better if I concentrated on my studies during term, if I do not, I might have to repeat a year. Think how much worse that would be for both of us."

"Yes my dearest, I know you are right; but it does seem so very hard."

"We can at least correspond, and before we know it we will be making plans in our letters for the Christmas vacation," he said, "when we can be together for five weeks. What times we shall have! Why it's almost worth doing without you for so long in order to cherish and love you the more when I return!" He was trying to make light of it, he knew, at the grave risk of seeming flippant.

"Yes, yes," she gasped, between passionate kisses, "and I shall love and cherish you all the more, too!"

The guard waved his flag and blew his whistle at this point and the train gave a convulsive jerk which caused their mouths to be separated. As the train pulled away, she was forced to step back.

She stood on the platform a picture of misery, then began to wave frantically, as if to make up for the time she had stood irresolute. He waved back and blew a kiss to her just before the train went round a curve and she was lost to sight.

Not long after this, he had settled into his rooms at the university and had entertained a few friends and acquaintances who had been undergraduates at the same time as he, when he noticed, for the first time, a strange young man who shared his staircase. He was immaculately dressed, but not in an English manner.

They nodded at one another when they encountered each other on the stairs or elsewhere, after this first encounter, but this familiarity did not as yet extend to the refectory, or anywhere else for that matter, because they had not yet been introduced. This fateful event occurred one evening at a poetry reading given in the rooms of a close friend of his.

"May I introduce a friend of mine to you?" this close friend enquired, just before the proceedings were to begin.

"By all means, my dear fellow," he replied.

"He is the dispossessed Count Charles de Braquelin who now resides near the Bois de Boulogne in Paris. Charles, this is my good friend Sir Roger Evesham."

"I am delighted to make your acquaintance," he replied, holding out his hand.

"*Bon soir*, Sir Roger," said the Count with a stiff little bow, after shaking hands. "I am delighted to make your acquaintance *aussi*.

The Count was a handsome young man of about his own age, Roger judged and roughly the same height; an inch or so over six feet. Fair-haired and with a slightly olive-skinned complexion. A luxuriant three-inch moustache, waxed at the tips, crowned his almost-feminine, smiling mouth with its even, white teeth. Roger's own moustache was sparse by comparison.

The Count's blue eyes sparkled with the same good-humour evident in his smile and the skin around them crinkled agreeably. He seemed all-in-all a most pleasant fellow.

"You are French, I take it?" said Roger, who was momentarily at a loss for something to say; the presence of the Count being somewhat overwhelming.

The Count laughed good-naturedly and the friend who had introduced them laughed, too. "You are making a little joke, yes?" said the Count when he had recovered his composure. "Assuredly, I am as French as I perceive you to be *Anglais*."

Roger was a little discomforted at so much laughter, he had been a fool to make such an enquiry, he realised, but he hadn't intended it to be a joke or a serious question, he had simply spoken without thinking.

His face must have fallen because Charles put his arm around his shoulders.

"No long faces, *mon ami*, as my *maman* used to say, but in French of course. It is of no consequence. *Alors*, let us sit next to each other, the poetry reading is about to begin.

Later, when he was alone in his rooms, Roger's thoughts dwelt on the Count and some of his attributes. First of all, his unfailing good humour seemed odd, considering his family had had the most extreme bad fortune to lose their chateau and lands in the Franco-Prussian war. If this ever happened to him (not that he seriously thought it could, this being England after all) he would never smile again!

The things which struck him almost as forcibly were the Count's depth and colour of speech and manner; he seemed so much more accomplished and experienced than he, even though the Frenchman was only a year older: 23 to his 22.

He had told a few humorous stories of his night-time adventures in the cafés and clubs of Paris with their glamorous, and not so glamorous, men and women and although he had not said so in as many words, it was obvious that he had more than a few emotional and physical entanglements with the girls and young women of the demi-monde who frequented these establishments.

He, Roger, had not experienced anything like this and his alliance with Lady Amelia was tame by comparison. The goodness and wholesomeness of their long-term relationship towered over the casual exploits of the Count, of course, but, nevertheless, he felt a tiny tinge of envy and hated himself for experiencing that emotion.

The Count when he was at home in Paris, if he was to be believed, regularly went to the Folies-Bergere theatre. Roger had heard of the Folies-Bergere and its scandalous shows which featured scantily-clad women and girls; he had been led to believe that only the lowest of the low went there, and here was a man who was a nobleman, albeit one dispossessed, talking of his visits to that vile place as casually as he might talk of a visit to his barber. It was a puzzle, the more so because the Count seemed to be in every other way a thoroughly decent man.

Roger had to confess, to himself at any rate he would not dream of mentioning it to anyone else, that he felt a certain curiosity concerning the undraped female form. He had never seen Amelia in any sort of state of undress; it was an understanding, an unspoken promise even, that that was for their wedding night and subsequent nights spent together.

He had been led to believe that the mystery which surrounded everything to do with the procreative act was better left just that - a mystery - until all was revealed in the nuptial bedchamber; also, that if this rule was not followed to the letter, then the most beautiful act which could take place between a man and a woman would be utterly desecrated.

Roger, with a start, came back to himself in the present time and saw that it was now past two o' clock. He threw his long-cold cigar stub into what remained of the fire got stiffly to his feet and went upstairs, where he made hasty preparations for bed.

EIGHT

The train was just pulling into Cannon Street station; it was ten minutes past eight on the evening of the 15th October and Roger was on his way to Black Dog Lane, Stepney to keep his mysterious appointment.

He had his fully-loaded Webley revolver with him and had practised with it the previous afternoon at the old archery butts. He had found that his proficiency was very much the same as the last time he took the revolver there; it was still very good, which was just as well; he might need to shoot quickly and accurately before the evening was out.

He had also brought with him the small mechanical device which he had made in his little workshop over the last few days. He had tested it many times; to ensure that it was completely reliable.

The four-wheeler cab rattled through the wet streets and pools of yellow light danced on the cobbles as the gas lamps flickered in the strong gusts of wind which the squally showers of rain created.

Roger had studied a street-map of the capital and had given the cabbie a destination which was a few hundred feet away from Black Dog Lane. He intended to alight at this destination and walk as quietly as possible to the address given in the letter; to this end he was wearing a pair of boots which had rubber soles.

He stood on a windy street corner and watched the cab rattle away into the distance. He was glad it was a cold, wet, windy evening because it would tend to keep the street urchins, loungers and unfortunate women indoors; he did not want to be troubled by anyone, he wanted to keep totally focused on the task in hand.

He adjusted his dripping bowler so that the brim came down to a level just above his eyes, checked his right and left pockets of his greatcoat for his pistol and mechanical device, respectively and began to walk silently down the road to the point where Black Dog Lane, branched from it.

He reached the entrance to Black Dog Lane, a cul-de-sac according to his map, and was a little surprised to find that it was no more than about four feet wide. It was flanked on one side by a warehouse and on the other by a dark, silent boot and shoe factory, so indicated by faded lettering on the wall which faced the gas-lit street and which had bars on its soot-grimed windows; perhaps it was no longer in business.

There were no gas lamps in Black Dog Lane, practically the only light came from the brightly-lit windows of a tavern towards the far end, about one hundred feet away. This was obviously a low establishment because, as he made his way cautiously down, he began to be aware of raucous male and hysterical female laughter punctuated by the occasional, presumably feminine, scream. As he approached the tavern he was just able to read the weathered sign which swung over the door: 'The Inn of the Black Dog'.

His silent progress up the lane was hampered by the quantities of domestic waste and worse which was liberally scattered over the whole surface. The smell of excrement was strong in his nostrils and he tried to breathe only through his mouth. The left side of the lane consisted of an unbroken very high wall down which rainwater streamed; probably the end wall of the factory building. The right side consisted of a row of cramped and crumbling two-storey hovels whose fronts gave directly onto the lane; only a few of these showed dimly-lit windows. He consulted his watch by the feeble light of one of the windows; it was five minutes to nine.

There was just enough light from the same source to read the numeral '12' roughly drawn in chalk on the leprous door of the next house; no light burned inside. Very quietly and quickly he fixed the rectangular frame of the mechanical device, via four right-angled tabs, to the door with the drawing-pins which he had brought for that purpose; this task was made easier by the fact that the wood of the door was soft with rot. The rain had by this time slackened to a steady drizzle.

He took from his jacket pocket a small piece of card around which was wound a six-foot length of manila fishing twine and carefully unravelled it. One end of the twine was attached to a ring at one end of a smooth metal pin, about four inches in length. Roger now silently inserted this pin into a small hole in the nearest side of the frame, at the same time holding two little hammers, which were free to swivel about a fixed rod which ran parallel to the pin, in an 'up' position with his other hand, the pin was then passed through another hole on the far side of the frame. The two hammers were now held in the 'up' position by the pin and Roger was able to take his hand from them and step to one side of the door, paying out the twine to its full extent as he did so.

Then, with his right hand on the revolver in his pocket, he gave the cord a firm but slow pull with his left. The hammers fell in quick succession giving the illusion that someone was administering two sharp raps to the door.

Hardly had the raps sounded when a rapid fusillade of six shots was heard from within the house and a part of the door roughly at the height of a human heart and of about the same area was violently pierced by six bullets from a heavy-calibre revolver, some ricocheting off the factory wall, opposite. The mechanical device, which had been fastened to the door at that height, was torn away by the emerging bullets and he heard it clattering down somewhere on the far side of the lane. The sudden, loud crashing sound of the shots, although he had been half-expecting it, had disoriented him slightly and he found himself swaying on his feet.

It had been a near thing, but before the tension which had been building within him could even begin to be dissipated by his safe deliverance from the hail of shots, the shattered door was flung back and a dapper, bearded man of medium height and build emerged, hatless and in shirt-sleeves, carrying a lantern which he shone on the ground outside the door; Roger listened to him cursing volubly at his lack of success and under cover of the sound took his revolver from his pocket, cocking it as he did so.

The man, who must have heard the click, fell silent, and cautiously shone his lantern over a slightly wider area. Very soon, the light from the lantern illuminated Roger standing silently with his revolver pointed at the other's head. At the same time, there suddenly arose a loud hubbub as a crowd of people, some bearing lanterns, came out of the tavern to investigate the noise.

The man was standing between the tavern and Roger and, after a moment's hesitation; he dropped the lantern and ran past Roger towards the street.

"Stop!" shouted Roger, "stop or I shall fire." But the man ran even faster and Roger was unable to carry out his threat, which would then have seemed cowardly. Instead, he started to give chase, but unfortunately stumbled over a large object lying in the rubbish which was everywhere present and almost fell. Before he could recover, the would-be assassin reached the corner where the lane and street intersected, tore around it, and disappeared.

Roger reached the street to find there was no sign of the man; there was not even the sound of someone running. He put away his gun and set off in the general direction of the station; he hoped that he would be able to hail a cab, soon. For the sake of discretion he had better not stay in this neighbourhood, he decided, let alone go back to the hovel where the man had been hiding; to see whether any clues had been left there. That activity would have to be left to the official police, who would not be long in arriving.

He heard raised voices, turned, and saw that the crowd from the tavern had followed him into the street; they shouted and gesticulated at him. He began to walk slowly towards them and made an impatient dismissive gesture at them, whereat they vacillated, came to a standstill and fell to whispering among themselves.

The consensus of this short debate must have been that he was an official of some kind; he was after all dressed like a gentleman, because they suddenly turned away as one man and went back towards the lane.

At length, as he walked down the street he was able to hail a cab to take him back to the station. No sooner had he seated himself in the cab than he had some kind of abreaction to the attempt to murder him, his head swam and he had to take a generous swig of brandy from his hip-flask. After that, he began to feel better; he sensed the blood beginning to course through his veins, once more.

He realised with some surprise that the attack had come when he had reached a place of safety - the cab - until then his nerves had been as taut as piano strings, but he had not even been aware of the fact.

The cab rolled up to the station and he paid the cabbie. Upon looking up the trains, he found that the next one which had a connection to his home station did not leave for more than an hour. He decided to have his supper in the restaurant of the station hotel; he felt in great need of sustenance. The hotel menu was likely to be rudimentary, but he didn't feel like traipsing around that part of London in search of something a bit more recherché; besides, he felt in the mood for plain food.

Accordingly, he sat down to a hearty meal of lamb loin chops, roast and boiled potatoes, peas and cabbage, a glass of porter to wash it down and a generous helping of treacle tart for dessert.

After he had eaten, he felt like a new man: a man who didn't have a care in the world. He realised that this feeling was predicated on the fact that he had cheated death and he also realised that it would not persist for very long.

He looked at his watch and saw that he did not have enough time to smoke a cigar at his table; no matter, he would smoke one on the train.

NINE

He woke in the early hours of the morning with a violent jolt of his whole body. He was able, for once, because of the sudden awakening, to recall the content of the dream which had caused it.

He was standing in the lane after the shots burst through the door, but this time, when the man emerged with the lantern, he must have reloaded his revolver because he pointed it at him, as soon as he was illuminated by the pool of light, and emptied it into him. It was this horrific event which caused him to move from the dreaming state to the state of being fully awake in a shaven second.

Roger took up the box of vestas he kept on his beside table and lit the candle which was there beside his hunter. He took up the hunter and upon pressing the winder to release the cover found that it was a quarter to six.

He knew that he would sleep no more that night; the dream had brought home to him the reality that might have been. Events could easily have taken that course and he would have been found dead by the denizens of the tavern.

He had to face up to the fact that a person or persons unknown wanted to murder him. Up until now he had somehow been able to leave this idea unformed in his mind and that had brought him some comfort. He was comfortable no longer and would not be until this new mystery was solved.

He realised that there was almost certainly some connection between what had happened and the secret work he was engaged in, but he did not want to dwell on that to any extent, for fear of losing his nerve. He was not going to let anything deflect him from his purpose.

It was at times like this that he missed Amelia most; they had always been able to tell each other their troubles. Her advice and sympathy had often been of great comfort to him and, he hoped and believed, his sympathy and advice had comforted her in at least equal measure.

He missed her terribly, even though she had turned out to be deeply flawed in the loyalty stakes.

He did not want to think of what followed, now, but could not help himself: he would never forget the day he realised that his childish affection for her had somehow been mysteriously transmuted into adult love and desire. It had all been so sudden.

He remembered that day chiefly because, for the first time since their early days, long ago, he felt awkward in her company; as if this was somehow wrong or bad and that they should no longer be allowed to spend time together, alone.

In fact, not long after that day, their respective parents formed similar opinions, despite being kept in the dark about the changed nature of their relationship. The truth seemed to have been conveyed to them by some mysterious process, somewhat akin to osmosis.

That day had dawned just like any other; they had made arrangements a few days earlier to go boating on Long Lake on the Evesham estate. They were to meet at two in the afternoon at the boathouse, unless the weather proved unsuitable; in the event, it turned out to be a beautiful July day.

But, as he dressed in white flannels and a straw boater after lunch, he felt a strange panic at the thought of being with her. When he turned the corner of the lane which led to the boathouse and saw her standing on the landing stage in a pink and white dress with matching bonnet and parasol, looking like a fashion plate, he had such an attack of fear that he would have turned around and gone back to his house, had she not seen him at the same moment.

He waved and shouted. "Hello Amelia!" but was unable to keep the nervousness out of his voice, despite trying on purpose, for some inexplicable reason, to be especially hearty.

"Hello Roger!" she shouted back. "Anything the matter?" She sounded puzzled.

She knew he wasn't his usual self! "No, I'm all right, thank you for asking. How are you?"

"I'm very well. Isn't it a lovely day for going out on the lake?"

"Yes, isn't it just?" He was at her side, now, and gave her a chaste kiss on her cheek in greeting, afterwards receiving one on his.

They had agreed to greet each other in this way about a year ago and both sets of parents had approved. But, now, the kisses, both given and received, seemed charged with electricity or fire, or perhaps both. How on earth was he going to get through the afternoon with her, without letting her know how unlike his usual self he was?

"I've brought the picnic hamper," she said, smiling at him in a way which seemed roguish, but which could simply be fancy on his part; his strange feelings were making him see everything about her in a new light, he realised.

He seemed to have some difficulty in taking his eyes away from her face in order to look at the hamper. Glancing quickly down, he saw it half-hidden behind her skirts.

"I'm very glad. I hope you didn't have to carry it all this way." Now he sounded stilted and unnatural.

"No. John carried it for me." She was still looking at him curiously, perhaps a reflection of the way he was looking at her; not having a mirror he had no way of knowing for certain.

Possibly, it had been his turn to bring a hamper, he surmised;

80

he was so confused he couldn't remember. He had learned, in his dealings with her that it was best to voice any feelings or misgivings he had, within reason of course, so that they would not grow into misunderstandings.

Sometimes, he had not done this, and the resulting confusion had cast a shadow over several days. They had always laughed about it afterwards, but such things grieved him. Part of the trouble lay in a reluctance, rooted in petty pride, to explain every little thing to her. She was so much better than he at coming forward with explanations for what might otherwise be taken for bad moods or sulkiness. On the whole, he felt he had better speak.

"Was it my turn to bring a hamper?" he asked, keeping his tone colourless and not meeting her eyes.

"Of course it wasn't," she said scornfully. "Neither of us would have brought one; if that were the case."

"I never thought of that," he said, and it was true that his consciousness and reason seemed to be clouded that afternoon. "I'm sorry." He briefly touched her hand in a placatory gesture and again experienced the fiery electricity.

"That's all right," she said, smiling, her eyebrows slightly raised at this new evidence of his derangement.

"I'll fetch the boat," he said, suiting the action to the word by quickly going into the boathouse to take down a boat and lower it into the water. He was glad to have an action to hide behind, especially as he was lost to her raised eyebrows during the performance of it.

This respite was short-lived, because all too soon they were ensconced in the boat, face to face, with the hamper stowed on the floor between them. However, he had managed to pull himself together a little.

He rowed while she steered and soon a light breeze which was blowing in their direction helped them on their journey to the centre of the lake.

She sat there with her parasol resting lightly on her shoulder, smiling at him, as pretty as a picture, and now that his initial nervousness had abated slightly, he was just about able to enjoy the sight.

They did not speak very much, perhaps because of the earlier awkwardness. It was possible that he was exaggerating the significance of this and their silence was simply something which always descended upon them until they moored as was their wont, in the centre of the lake for their picnic. On this curious, strangely disordered afternoon, he was once again at a loss to remember.

They moored at their favourite spot at a point roughly equidistant from the two nearest shores, using his improvised anchor of a large stone tied to a length of line. They had begun doing this at a much earlier time in their relationship, when they had both evinced a morbid dread of eavesdroppers, and had done so ever since. As events turned out it was as well they did so this time, also.

They bustled about in a well-worn routine in which each knew exactly what he or she had to do in order to set out the picnic things with the minimum of wasted time or effort and without getting in each other's way or rocking the boat excessively.

Soon, they sat facing one another each with greaseproof paper packets of sandwiches resting on napkins on their laps. They did not stand on ceremony and began eating. After he had eaten two chicken sandwiches one ham and one cheddar cheese, he felt a lot better. The little tin kettle was singing on the spirit stove and everything felt almost as usual. Until she spoke.

"I know what's the matter with you and what you are feeling," she said with the most frank and sensible expression on her face that he had ever seen. A sudden breeze blew at this point which ruffled her skirts and briefly exposed her calves;

this made him uncomfortably aware of how thin the material was.

Although he felt that he knew what she was going to say, he said: "how can you possibly know what I am feeling?"

"I can give you the long answer or the short answer. Which would you like to hear first?"

He said, or rather heard himself saying, because his voice momentarily seemed very far away: "the long."

"Well then, I have to tell you that we girls are not fools where these things are concerned. Most of the time, in fact, we are much better informed than boys. We learn things from our mothers at a young age which prepare us for the truth about life, love and what might be termed the physical side of a relationship."

He was, quite simply, shocked to hear a girl of sixteen speak of such things, the fact that she was his girl did not make it any better or easier to bear; nor did the fact that he was only sixteen himself. He felt that the conversation had taken a turn from which there could be no easy escape. At that point the kettle boiled over and he mechanically poured the hot water onto the leaves in the teapot and, with some difficulty because his hands were shaking, put the lid in place. His throat was dry, but he managed to say without meeting her gaze: "and the short."

"I feel exactly the same way about you."

He was so astonished that he could only stare at her open-mouthed. A long silence followed during which the anxiety at his response to this registered more and more in her face.

"You are not supposed to - you are not meant to," he managed to say, haltingly, at last.

"I am not meant to want you in the way you so obviously want me. Is that what you mean?"

"Yes," he said, very quietly. His ears had suddenly become hot, as if her last words had scalded them.

"Stuff and nonsense! So typical of a man to expect only spiritual love from a woman whereas he feels physical and spiritual love for her!"

"I am only a boy!" he almost shouted, stung by her words.

"And when you are a man, what then?"

"We are too young to speak of such things," he said defensively and half-ashamedly.

"If we are old enough to feel desire for each other, then the sooner we speak of it, the better."

He remained silent; in the hope that if they spoke no more then things would revert to the way they had always been. He hoped in vain because she soon tried a different tack.

"When we say we love each other, as we occasionally do," here she looked heavenwards in a gesture of derision, "what meaning does it have for you?"

"Well," he mumbled, disconcerted by her mocking gesture, "it means that I am fond of you and that you have a place in my heart, as I hope I have in yours."

"Is that all?" she seemed angry, now.

"Up until today, that was all, yes."

For some reason, these words had a calming effect on her, the tension rapidly left her body and she smiled at him.

"So you have woken out of your boyhood, at last?"

"Yes, I think I must have."

"And what have you to say now?"

"I love you completely and I want always to be with you."

"Yes?" she prompted.

"I want to marry you; when we are older."

"Good," she said, smiling more broadly, "I will not have to belabour you about the head with the boathook after all." Seeing what must have been a look of terror on his face, she went on: "I was only jesting."

This, last, was not very convincing.

"Why would you feel the need to even contemplate such a thing?" he asked, genuinely distressed, "let alone speak it."

"You are a fool Roger, where the language of love and devotion is concerned, but no worse, I am sure, than the next man. I would only have beaten you around the head with the boathook if you had not mentioned marriage. You have a lot to learn about women and I shall, in the fullness of time, endeavour to teach you."

"I am not at all certain that I want to be your pupil, now that I know how ruthless you are!" He was not serious, and something in his face must have given him away, because she burst into laughter and he quickly joined in. The laughter seemed to end the seriousness which had crept into their afternoon together, and he hoped that they could now go back to simply enjoying each other's company as they had always done; even though some part of him knew that their relationship had just moved several steps away from that childish perspective.

Roger came to himself with a start; judging by the amount the candle had burned down, he must have been in his reverie for some time. Although he did not approve of smoking in his bedroom, he rose to collect his cigar case from the inside pocket of his jacket, hanging in the dressing room, and went back to the bedroom where, sitting on the bed, he lit the cigar with the candle. He felt the need of this particular vice, just now.

TEN

It was the morning of the following Monday and Roger was entrained on the eight o' clock for London; he had an appointment to see the prime minister, who warned him in his hastily-scribbled note that he would only be able to grant him a 'very few minutes' at ten, for the purpose of handing in his preliminary report.

He sat looking out of the window of the first class carriage as the fields, whitened by an early winter frost, went rolling by. Here and there, in little groups huddled together for warmth under the bare trees, stood some unhappy looking dairy cows; their breathing marked by puffs of white vapour; also, one or two unhappy horses.

After he had been to Downing Street, he intended to take an early luncheon and then spend several hours at the British Museum reading room in an attempt to identify or classify the horseshoe device. It was a tenuous clue which might have been drawn in an idle moment and prove to have no bearing on the solution of the task in hand, but he could leave no stone unturned. He heartily wished he could have discovered its meaning, if any, in time to include that information in his report, which was much too sparse for his liking, despite the considerable number of hours he had spent working on it.

When he was ushered into the prime minister's office Roger could see that the statesman wore a tired and harassed air. But, despite this, he seemed very glad to see Roger. And after he had carefully placed the folder containing the report on his desk, listened patiently to his carefully-rehearsed short account of his doings (these didn't include the murder attempt) kindly enquired of him what his itinerary for the day might be, shook his hand just before he took his leave and wished him Godspeed, once again.

Because the day was fine and dry Roger decided to walk to the Café Royal, where he was going to have at least two cups of coffee and, a little later, luncheon, but he was going to keep a weather eye open for Sanderson, and if he turned out to be present after a preliminary scout around, then he would find some other café or restaurant in which to have lunch.

As he walked along, he felt more and more uncomfortable. It was not that he felt he was being watched and followed by someone, exactly, but the feeling was akin to it; he had to fight off a strong desire to turn around and see who was walking behind him. He realised that the encounter in Stepney was going to play on his nerves every time he was out and about in London, until this affair was brought to a successful conclusion.

He turned into the Café Royal, grateful for its eternal bustle and bright lights, the clattering of cutlery on fine china and the sound of dozens of conversations going on at the same time. Nevertheless, he asked for a corner table so that he could covertly observe the other diners and at the same time make it more difficult to be covertly observed by them. He was anxious to dispel the remnants of his earlier anxiety. Luckily, Sanderson was noticeable by his absence.

His coffee arrived and he took the opportunity, while he held up his cup to sip it, to look over it and see if anyone in particular was taking any interest in him, but there was no one. After drinking his coffee he took out his cigar case and sat smoking until he was ready to order luncheon. This was not long because the coffee and nicotine sharpened his appetite.

As he ate his salmon, he shot quick glances into every part of the dining area, but, again, he didn't seem to be the focus of anyone's gaze. He realised that the main reason he was nervous was that the man who had tried to kill him had given every appearance of being a gentleman and would therefore be capable of blending unobtrusively into the clientele of a place like this.

Having finished his lunch, he came out of the café, turned left and started to walk in the direction of Bloomsbury. In truth, he was not looking forward to his research work at the library, he would much sooner go to the park, stroll around to see if he could find someone he knew, have a conversation, share a cigar or two with whomever it turned out to be, and go home with the fruits of the conversation and the sights and sounds of London still running around inside his head.

Just as he was crossing the road, his destination being on the far side, a girl on a bicycle went whizzing past him, almost knocking him down. He stared after her but she did not so much as acknowledge him with a backward glance. He shrugged and went on until he gained the safety of the pavement. One or two passers-by looked at him oddly. His face must still show the shock he felt at his narrow escape.

He reached the British Museum and went to the reading room desk. He was an accredited reading room ticket holder and so all he had to do was to give a copy of the horseshoe design to the official and explain what information he was seeking. After a short exchange, the man indicated a nearby desk and invited Roger to sit there so that as many books as were deemed relevant could be brought to him by the assistants.

After what seemed a considerable time, but which was probably no more than twenty minutes, an assistant brought half-a-dozen or so books for him to peruse. Some books had the relevant sections indicated by enclosed slips of paper; other books had a much more diffuse approach to the subject and these were by far the more tedious to work with, because every page had to be examined for any possible information.

As he worked, another few books were brought and the ones he had finished with were taken away; and this relay system went on all afternoon and early evening, until at last there were no more volumes which could possibly be helpful to his quest. He had brought with him a pocket-sized notebook; some sharpened pencils and an eraser, but at the end of the day the pages of the notebook were almost as pristine as when he arrived. He had found only one illustration, originating from somewhere in Polynesia, which was vaguely reminiscent of the horseshoe design from the poetry book, and this he had faithfully copied onto a page in his notebook together with the few facts about it which were available. He tipped the assistants and the desk official and left with a heavy heart; because he had so little to show for all those hours in the reading room.

It was dark when he got outside but he nevertheless decided to walk to Charing Cross for his train home; he had been sitting too long in the musty atmosphere of the reading room and wanted to get some exercise before he spent another hour and a half sitting in train carriages.

All went well until he crossed High Holborn and then he realised he was being followed. It had not been apparent in the more crowded thoroughfares but now he was certain. The man behind him was being very careful but he had given himself away once or twice at corners and junctions. Roger was unarmed, but he was determined to confront his pursuer; accordingly, he walked more quickly until he had put about a hundred feet or more between them, then he turned down a narrow unlit alley off Covent Garden and pressed himself silently into a doorway.

The entrance to the alley was fairly well lit and within a few seconds Roger saw a man stop and hesitate for a few moments before coming down towards him.

Roger was well-concealed in the doorway, the only difficulty was his breath, which formed a cloud of vapour in the cold, still air; he controlled it as best he could by breathing out through a crevice in the door which stood just behind him.

As the man drew level, Roger could see that he held a pistol of some kind in his hand at about the level of his waist. When he had gone a few steps past Roger's place of concealment the baronet jumped out and thrust the unopened folding pocket-knife he had used to sharpen his pencils into the small of the other man's back, hoping that the unknown man would assume it was the barrel of a pistol.

"Keep perfectly still," hissed Roger, "or I swear I will kill you." The man stood stock still.

"Now drop your weapon." The man complied and the gun fell at his feet. With a slight amount of contortion Roger retrieved it while keeping the pocket-knife tightly against the man's back.

"Put your hands up and turn to face me," commanded Roger and the man sulkily obeyed. The light from the street fell on the man's crestfallen face with its mutton-chop whiskers and Roger estimated he was only a little older than himself. The man was fairly well-dressed but was somewhat down at heel; it showed most in his slightly battered bowler.

"Now tell me who you are and why you were following me," Roger demanded, pointing the revolver at the man's chest.

"I am Inspector Henry Sullivan of Scotland Yard," the man replied after some hesitation.

Roger felt a rush of relief and a sudden lessening of tension. But was obliged to voice his scepticism. "I don't believe you," he said.

"If I may," said the man gesturing with his chin down at his right breast.

"Very well," said Roger, nodding his assent.

The man took a leather case a little smaller than a wallet out of his inside breast pocket and silently handed it to Roger. On opening it and examining the card which lay behind a piece of yellowing, grimy celluloid, within, by the light of a match, keeping the pistol aimed at his captive the while, Roger could see it was a genuine warrant card of the plain clothes division.

"All right," said Roger, as he handed back the case, "let us say you are who you say you are; it does not explain your actions. Perhaps, we can begin with your account of those. I shall retain the revolver for the moment."

"First of all," said the alleged inspector, can I lower my arms?"

"Yes."

"Secondly, I know who you are. You are Sir Roger Evesham."

"How on earth do you know that?"

"Because the prime minister's office requested Scotland Yard to detail an officer of the rank of inspector to watch over you today. I am the second inspector to do so. I changed shifts with my colleague outside the British Museum."

"How did Scotland Yard know where to find me?"

"You may recall that the prime minister requested your itinerary, when you were with him this morning."

"Of course. How stupid of me; it is obvious now, in the light of what you have just told me, that you are genuine, please take back your revolver."

"Thank you, Sir Roger." The inspector took back the pistol, put up the safety catch, uncocked it and secreted it in his overcoat pocket. "Have you put up the safety on your gun, Sir Roger?" he enquired.

"I am unarmed, inspector," said Roger with a smile, at the same time motioning with the pocket-knife, as if it were a pistol. The inspector blinked rapidly, but said nothing.

"Why did you follow me into the alley with a cocked revolver? Roger enquired.

"Purely for your protection, Sir Roger," said the inspector in an official tone. "If someone had jumped out at you, I would have been ready for him."

"Why does the prime minister believe I need police protection?"

"I don't know that, Sir Roger, I only follow the orders of my superiors."

"Surely you can tell me something more than that?"

"I can't, sir."

"I'll tell you what is on my mind, inspector, I have a little proposition to make to you."

"What might that be, sir?" The inspector sounded suspicious.

"You tell me what you know, and I shall forget I ever saw you this evening. Then, you'll be able to put in a nice, uncomplicated report to your superiors."

There was a lengthy pause before the inspector spoke. "You're a card I must say, sir, but I still don't see as how I can." His uncertainty seemed to have affected his grammar.

"Come on man! I give you my word that anything you tell me will be held in the strictest confidence. Here, shake hands on it." The inspector reluctantly shook his hand.

"All right, Sir Roger, you win. Intelligence has been received, at the highest level, that you are not safe when alone in the City."

"The highest level - the prime minister?"

"I can't say any more than that, sir."

"Very well, I shan't press you. In any case, I think it's time to say good evening."

"I've to see you safely onto your train, sir."

"Must you?"

"Yes, sir," he bridled.

"Very well, we'll walk down to Charing Cross together."

The inspector made an explosive sound. "I can't do that Sir Roger; you're not even supposed to know I'm watching you!"

"What then?"

"You go on your way, sir. I won't be far behind."

As he got on his train, he glanced around and was just in time to see the inspector concealing himself behind a pile of luggage. He was very tempted to wave, but the imp in him was checked at the last moment by the knowledge that the threat to his life was still very real.

It was odd though, he reflected, as the train rattled homewards, he had felt that he was being watched for most of the day, but had not caught anyone in the act, so to speak, until after he left the British Museum. But, then he remembered the inspector had told him that he had changed shifts with his colleague outside that institution. The man who had followed him earlier had obviously been much more skilled.

There was one question to which he wished he had the answer: what secret information had prompted the prime minister to engage the inspectors to watch over him that day?

He thought hard for some minutes. If he was in imminent danger, the prime minister would explicitly have told him so when he saw him that morning; of that he was certain. So, the information held by the prime minister must be speculative, at best. No more than interdepartmental gossip? Perhaps a bit more than that, but not much.

Roger fell to wondering if news of the murder attempt had reached the prime minister's office. But surely that was impossible? Oh well, he probably never would know, one way or another; but at least, the events of the day meant that he had a lot more confidence in the prime minister's ability to keep him out of serious trouble.

He arrived home tired and surprisingly hungry. He had arranged, before he left, for a cold supper of cheddar cheese sandwiches to be left in the small dining room, together with a couple of bottles of light ale.

Accordingly, after removing and hanging up his overcoat and jacket, he had a wash and went to the room where he often dined alone.

The kitchen staff had surpassed themselves, not only were there cheese sandwiches, there were some roast beef and some ham. There were three bottles of ale and two of wine, one red and one white; there was even the remains of a fire in the grate; he stirred it into a blaze with the poker and added some coal.

He sat at the table, placed the napkin in his lap and began with the cheese sandwiches. As he ate, he quickly realised he would never be able to eat all that had been set out, so he decided to eat one of each variety of sandwich in turn, then, beginning again at the first plate, repeat the process until he felt replete. He decided not to have any wine, for fear of indigestion in the night, and resolved to have it relaced in his cellar first thing in the morning.

After he had eaten, he slumped down into one of the two armchairs, lit a cigar and sat gazing into the revived fire. He was pleasantly tired and whenever he felt this way, late at night, when the house was silent, he found that he could see images of the day in the flickering flames.

He saw the face of the prime minister speaking silently to him across his desk, he saw the people in the café, he saw the discomfited face of the inspector and then he saw the haughty girl on a bicycle who had almost knocked him down in the street near the British Museum, with her head in the air and with a number of books in a small basket fixed to the front of the handlebars; probably a student of the university. She had been wearing one of those shocking divided skirts, about which there had been all that talk, some years earlier.

The divided skirts had divided the nation, he recalled, smiling to himself. And what was more, in some ways the division remained, because there were still factions whose members were either for or against their use. Debates were still being held in drawing rooms across the land and they could still become quite heated; especially when they involved young female relatives who wanted to take up bicycle riding.

Almost all the women, and quite half of the men, had been of the opinion that women who wore divided skirts on a bicycle, or anywhere else for that matter, were no better than fallen. Divided skirts had been seen as the invention of the devil himself, with only one purpose: to inflame the unbridled lust of men.

Seeing that girl on a bicycle that afternoon, wearing a divided skirt, reminded him of the row there had been when Amelia had wanted to take up the ordinary bicycle for women, which had been adapted from the ordinary bicycle for men by the simple expedient of changing the position of the crossbar between saddle and handlebar swivel.

He had become enamoured with bicycles at the same time as Amelia and was given one by his father as a sort of advanced fifteenth birthday present, so that he could accompany Amelia on bicycle rides on roads belonging to one or other of the two adjoining estates. Both sets of parents thought it best that they did not venture out onto public roads until they were reasonably proficient.

There were several, long, level roads within the two estates to practise on, and so neither of the two children anticipated any difficulties on that score. However, difficulties, or rather one specific difficulty, quickly arose within days of their beginning to ride.

He had been taking lessons from his father for a few days until he was able to manage on his own. Arrangements were then made for him to instruct Amelia in the esoteric art of bicycling. The difficulty arose because her parents had absolutely forbidden her to use divided skirts, with the result that she frequently got her skirt, and or, petticoats caught up in the chain.

At best, this meant trouble for her at home when she returned with oily streaks on or around the hem area of her skirt or petticoat, and at worst she was thrown over the handlebars when her skirt jammed and the bicycle came to an abrupt halt. Whenever this occurred she sustained superficial injuries, including bruises, grazed hands and knees and on one occasion a grazed cheekbone; neither of the two bicycles being possessed of the later development of the ratcheted rear-wheel sprocket.

It said much for Amelia that she persevered, despite everything. She tried bundling her skirt up with cord or ribbons, but the movement of her legs always caused it to free itself and catch in the chain, once more.

In the end, Amelia being Amelia, she managed to purchase, by stealth, two divided skirts and would change into one or other of them, behind bushes, or any suitable screen which presented itself, before beginning proceedings, they would then enjoy a trouble-free afternoon's cycling and she would change back into her conventional skirt before going home.

All went well until the inevitable happened: she was caught red-handed cycling in a divided skirt by her father; who became quite incandescent with rage with the two of them and who subsequently accompanied Amelia home on foot; this mode of transport, while wearing a divided skirt, being considered less bad than cycling while wearing one (by a small margin).

Roger, he was only Roger, at that time, wended his way home slowly and not a little tearfully. He, like Amelia, wheeled his bicycle along beside him; he had lost interest in riding it. As he walked along, the usual questions crowded through his head: would he ever see Amelia again? Would they ever be able to cycle together again? They had had such wonderful times, and so on.

When he got home, it was not long before a servant from Hindthorpe Hall arrived bearing a note from Lord Hindthorpe for Roger's father. Roger was summoned to his father's study and an altercation ensued which did not last very long, because, although Roger was theoretically at fault for not informing someone in authority at Hindthorpe Hall of Amelia's reprehensible behaviour, his father, who knew how headstrong Amelia could be, did not believe his son was seriously blameworthy and did not, therefore, resort to corporal punishment; merely declaring that Roger was officially in disgrace for three days and confined to the house.

Since the worst part of this was the fact that he was confined to the house at a time when Amelia was unable to see him, anyway, together with early bedtimes and certain dietary restrictions, Roger did not find this punishment too onerous.

The three days passed, then another three, and still he didn't see or hear anything from anybody about Amelia. He worried about her and missed her a lot. His greatest fear was that she would be 'sent away' a fate which she herself feared more than anything and which had only been threatened by her otherwise doting parents when all other attempts at correction had failed.

Then, some days later, when he had all but given up hope of ever setting eyes on her again, she called for him at the front door with her bicycle and wearing a divided skirt!

"What happened?" he asked her breathlessly, when they had cycled sufficiently far from the house not to be overheard by anyone.

"I made them see sense," she replied, simply, with a beatific smile.

Thinking of this, now, in the present day, made Roger smile a little.

ELEVEN

Roger came back from church on the following Sunday resolving not to attend services there in the foreseeable future.

Charles had made one of his sporadic appearances at a time when Amelia was also present and although they took great pains not to show it and had sat in different parts of the church, their mutual admiration and affection had been obvious to him in the glances they shot each other from time to time; he knew them both so very well. There were times when his sadness at this turn of events was almost overwhelming, disconcerting him for days and days. And yet, he mused, as he sat at the desk in his study that afternoon, Charles had been his best friend when they were up at Oxford together.

Smoking and drinking, they had often talked late into the night at one or the other's rooms on all kinds of subjects, setting the world to rights and once or twice airing personal grievances and confidences which he, Roger, for one, would not have been able to countenance with any other friend or personal acquaintance.

No doubt the brandy brought down barriers and it, together with the intimacy which developed during the small hours when all was quiet, very often appeared to encourage the mutual baring of souls. But, it was more than that; it was as if they loved each other like brothers who were on the best possible terms.

This love was never openly expressed or even acknowledged, but it was there, and this was the very reason that seeing him, now, after that terrible betrayal of his, Roger's, utmost trust, was very nearly more than he could bear; hence his painful decision that morning.

One subject, which had they had discussed at Oxford, a very inappropriate one to consider on a Sunday, after church, Roger realised with some shame, was brought back to mind after the shock of seeing the interaction between Charles and Amelia: the physical aspect of a man's relationship with a woman.

He, Roger, must have been further into his cups than was usual or he would certainly not have been so drawn on the subject. But, worse, much worse, was the ordeal he was later subjected to; partly because he had admitted to Charles that he did not feel that he was yet a whole man because of his total lack of experience in that direction; partly because of bravado; partly because he wanted extra fellowship with the Frenchman.

"But you don't mean to tell me that you have never known a woman in that way!" Charles had exclaimed with incredulity written all over his handsome features.

"No, I have not," he had mumbled.

"Not even with the fair Amelia, of whose beauty I have heard so much and to whom you are betrothed?" Charles' incredulity seemed to increase and his face became a study of disbelief.

"Especially not her," Roger said, hotly.

"Tell me *mon ami*," said Charles, his eyes twinkling over his brandy glass, "you are possessed of normal feelings for women?"

"Yes, I am," said Roger, more hotly than before.

"Including the fair Amelia?"

Roger took a gulp of brandy. "Of course I include Amelia in what I have said."

"But she is an Englishwoman of high birth and impeccable morals, yes?"

"I think you begin to understand," said Roger with something like relief.

"But you have female servants, don't tell me you have not been tempted to, how shall I say, press them into a different kind of service?"

Roger was minded to use strong language, but, instead, said mildly; "you don't know the English aristocracy very well, Charles, I must say. That sort of thing may happen in the circles you move in, but it almost never happens here."

"But I have read novels about English milords and their antics with some of their young and attractive maids," his eyes danced and he almost laughed. It was clear to Roger that the other's side of the conversation had descended into teasing.

"Novels like that are like all novels: works of fiction. But those in particular are written by filthy-minded hacks who have no shame and no respect for the ruling classes of this country. No good could possibly ever come from such liaisons, only scandal, execration and shame."

Charles laughed out loud. "Our countries are indeed very different, I can say from my own experiences with servant-girls, when I was on the brink of manhood and beyond, that that sweet mystery, of which we have just spoken, was unravelled for me and the girls did not suffer; instead, they were rewarded."

Roger was disgusted and the disgust must have shown in his face for the eyes of his friend twinkled at his discomfiture.

"Do not despise me *mon ami*, the meat of one country is the poison of another *n'est pas?*"

"That's certainly one way of putting it!"

"And if I told you that there exists a celebrated establishment not far from here which caters for high-born young men, especially those who are students of this university, who, how shall I say? have led the sheltered life, due to their good upbringing, and are now at something of a loss where such matters are concerned; what would you say?"

"You mean to tell me that you know of a high-class brothel in the district where trollops, who are not actually illiterate, sell their favours to formerly inviolate young gentlemen, so that they can become sexually awakened?"

"*Oui!*"

"I would say that the alcohol has fuddled your brain so that you are not rational; otherwise, you would never have so much as mentioned such an establishment in my presence. I would never allow myself to be seen dead within even a mile of such a place."

"Absolute discretion is their watchword, *mon ami*," he said, without a trace of humour showing in his face. He was obviously in deadly earnest.

"We have stayed up too late and smoked and drunk too much. I think we should call it a night," said Roger.

And that, for the present, was where the matter rested. At that time Roger believed him to be depraved and perhaps a little mad, but, in the end, he put the whole thing down to the natural conflict which often arises between men of different nations concerning their different customs and practices.

About a week passed and they were sitting up late in Charles' rooms smoking and drinking, best of friends again, when the subject of the local brothel recurred, but this time the Frenchman approached it from a different tack.

"Have you ever tried to envisage the actual sequence of events concerning the marriage bed on the first night of your honeymoon?" he enquired.

As a matter of fact, Roger had indeed been thinking about that particular night a great deal more, partly because of their last conversation, but mainly because the wedding was to take place in August and it was now late May. It was beginning to prey on his mind; what if he made a complete fool of himself on that night of all nights?

"Would it not be better, *mon ami*," Charles went on, "for us to journey to the place I mentioned, so that you can at least make your essay into that function of the husband in an impersonal atmosphere to, perhaps, spare yourself and the fair Amelia any possible embarrassment in the future?"

Charles had spoken of this difficult topic with tact and complete understanding. Gone, now, was the mocking demeanour he had displayed on the previous occasion when the house of ill-repute had been discussed.

"After all, the establishment is there for that reason *precisement*, yes?"

"Yes. Yes. I dare say," said Roger, a trifle too curtly. "The trouble with you, Charles, is that you are so damned reasonable and convincing about something I am far from certain is the right course. After you leave here, you really should consider a career in politics."

"*Mais oui, mon cher* Roger, that is what I intend to do. Assuredly. I hope one day to be *President de France*." He laughed in a very engaging manner and Roger felt a release of the tension which had been building in him.

"Hang it all, Charles, I cannot do it! No matter what you say, I shall never darken the door of that evil place; I shall never consent to meet the especially trained ladies of the night who frequent it, much less share a bed with any one of them!"

"*Alors!* two then, perhaps, *mon cher?*"

"You are impossible, tonight," said Roger, laughing. "I think I had best avoid you for the rest of term, lest perdition surely befall this representative of the House of Evesham!"

"That is up to you, *mon ami*," he said, shrugging his shoulders and making a long face. "But, there is not much term left and so the opportunity will soon be lost; perhaps forever."

And there, once again, the matter rested.

In the event, it was Roger who approached Charles concerning a visit to the brothel. This was only a week before the going-down ball.

The fact that Lady Amelia was travelling up to Oxford to

stay with relatives and be his dance partner for the evening had prompted him into doing something about his marriage-bed horrors, at last.

And so, on the evening in question, Charles and Roger began by dining out of college in an intimate little restaurant in the town which was not considered fashionable by the dining cognoscenti of the university, this was intentional and they wore nothing which would mark them out as undergraduates; they wanted to preserve their anonymity throughout the evening.

Roger had been very nervous throughout the day about the ordeal, as he saw it, which lay before him and had slept badly the night before.

The relaxed meal with some, but not too much wine, was Charles' idea; Roger had been all for going directly to the house, which was quite a few miles out, at Thame, and leaving as soon as was reasonably practical, afterwards. Charles was totally opposed to this bull at a gate attitude at any and all stages of the evening to come. The last thing one wanted to convey when one went to such a place was anything other than complete insouciance, he said. Roger, who had no idea of the proper form, was forced to bow to Charles' greater experience and better judgement.

After they had been in the restaurant for a while and had eaten some food and drunk a couple of glasses of wine, Roger began to relax and he was forced to concede that Charles had been right, about this part of the proceedings at any rate, and this in turn helped him to believe he was right about everything that was to follow.

At length, they finished their meal and covered their tracks further by walking some distance from the restaurant before engaging the finest four-wheeler they could find; so as to make the best possible impression on arrival, they set off for the house of ill-repute in Thame.

This turned out to be a surprisingly grand house in a very good state of repair; standing in its own grounds with a long carriage-drive which passed under a pillared portico with steps leading to an imposing main entrance with double doors. The semicircular segmented fanlight revealed a soft light burning within. The house did not seem to have any identifying features; neither name nor number appeared anywhere.

Charles pulled gently at the ornate bell-pull, footsteps which were unquestionably feminine were heard approaching and the door opened with a frou-frou of skirts to reveal a middle-aged woman wearing a black gown of lustrous bombazine with several flounces. She had obviously been beautiful once because traces of it were still evident.

It was at this point that Roger's carefully-garnered insouciance fled, leaving him almost staggering with amazement; for the bombazine-clad woman greeted Charles effusively, embracing him warmly, kissing him on both cheeks and addressing him both as Charles and 'Monsieur Le Comte'. Charles had obviously been here before and probably more than once.

Roger was introduced by Charles to the woman, who a little later proved to be the madam, simply as 'Sir Roger'. Charles explained that only first names and titles, if any, were used by the clientele.

The madam bowed gravely to each of them in turn and showed them into a large, luxuriantly-appointed sitting room where there seemed to be a preponderance of couches and chaise longues against one wall, as opposed to only a few armchairs ranged towards the middle of the room, in front of them. A subtle light was provided by a few lamps ranged around the room.

The madam left them and they were alone in the room. Charles selected an armchair and indicated that his friend should sit in the one next to it. Roger took this opportunity, now that he had recovered somewhat, to remonstrate with Charles.

"Why did you not tell me that you had been here before?" he hissed under his breath.

Charles smiled serenely and charmingly at him. "Would it have made you feel any more relaxed, if I had told you about my previous visit?"

"Visits," interjected Roger, with a grimace.

Charles smile broadened and he bowed his head. "Very well, *mon cher ami*, visits. As I was about to say, if I had told you about my previous visits, you would have plagued me with your questions; my answers would have discomposed you, even more than you are now discomposed and you would never have consented to come. Is that not so?"

Roger considered this for a few moments and conceded inwardly that Charles was probably in the right of it. How well Charles seemed to know him; and everybody else for that matter! He nodded, silently, even a little shamefacedly, and felt himself relax a little.

"That's better," said Charles, seeing acquiescence in Roger's face.

"Yes," said Roger, "I will allow that, as far as this place is concerned, the less I know about what goes on here, the better."

Just at that moment, a door which had previously been unremarked by Roger, since it had seemed to be only an ornate panel, one of many in the wall opposite, opened at a point where there was a gap in the row of couches and chaise longues and the madam entered followed by several young and pretty women all dressed in gowns having a great deal of décolletage, so that, in each case, a considerable expanse of their ample breasts was freely displayed.

The madam clapped her hands and the women formed themselves into a row in front of the two men. The madam clapped her hands again and the women each began to turn slowly in circles on the spot, like dancers; there was a strong fragrance of a mixture of perfumes. Roger was mesmerised by their movements and was slightly disappointed when the madam clapped her hands once more and they all came to rest facing them, smiling red-painted smiles and with their faces slightly flushed under the powder they each wore, somewhat pointlessly thought Roger; because they were all of an age when they needed neither paint nor powder to make them look attractive. But then, he remembered he was in a bawdy house, albeit one of a better class, and that the rules to which he was accustomed could not be applied.

One of the young women, wearing an emerald gown, unfortunately bore a very strong facial resemblance to Amelia and he found himself staring at her until her smile broadened; at which he quickly looked elsewhere.

The madam clapped her hands, yet again, and all the women, including the madam herself, seated themselves on the couches and chaise longues. All the young women wore their hair piled high on their heads and one or two took out small hand mirrors which they had secreted in their bosoms and groomed their coiffures a little; tucking any loose ends into the mass.

The courtesans all seemed to have mastered the art of smiling tirelessly and a little archly, as if they knew secrets unknown to women in general; Roger conceded that this was very probable.

His own jaw was aching with the effort of smiling pleasantly and he was vaguely aware that something was expected of him, but he was not sure what, when Charles dug him in the ribs and whispered to him that he must choose one of them, but must not on any account reveal his choice to anyone at this time. Charles whispered to him, by way of example, that he had chosen the woman in blue and for some inexplicable reason Roger felt pleased and relieved he had not chosen the woman in the emerald dress.

This, the choosing of a woman for the sport which was to follow and then indicating this choice, afterwards, was facilitated by the fact that no two gowns worn by the women were of the same colour.

After a little while, during which no impatience was shown by anyone, Roger chose a blonde, slightly-plump, petite young woman, wearing a very fetching champagne coloured gown; mainly because he felt that she had a kind face and would hopefully, therefore, be tolerant of the almost complete ignorance which he would be obliged to reveal to her, on reaching her room.

At length, the madam looked at them interrogatively, and when both men nodded their heads, stood and clapped her hands once more. At this, the women also stood, then curtseyed and filed out through the door. After they had all departed, the madam closed the door softly behind them and asked the two friends to tell her whom they favoured.

When they had each done so, using the colour of the woman's dress as a guide, she nodded, smiled, and said "Rose and Edith." "Rose for you, monsieur," nodding at Charles, "and Edith for you, sir," nodding at Roger. "Perhaps," she went on, looking at each in turn, "Monsieur Charles could show his friend where the girls' rooms are and by so doing save my poor old legs?"

"*Certainement, Madame*," Charles replied with a bow. If you would follow me, Sir Roger?" He led the way out through the door by which they had entered the room. An age, seemingly, had passed since then.

Charles led the way up the stairs past two landings and down a long corridor which led off the third landing. Here, about half way down, were a number of doors which had oval porcelain plaques fixed to them. These plaques depicted posies of flowers of different colours and Roger saw one which only had a sprig of green leaves, clearly, the colour themes of the girls' dresses were continued via these plaques.

Charles indicated a plaque which had pale yellow flowers on it, mimed a knock on the door, went down the corridor where he knocked on the door of the girl of his choice, paused, presumably for her to invite him to enter and went in, closing the door softly behind him.

Without hesitation, Roger knocked at his girl's door; he knew that if he stopped to think about his actions he was lost. On hearing the girl say 'come in' he entered.

The girl was sitting at her dressing table, on the far side of the room, taking pins from her hair and placing them in a little glass dish. She smiled a radiant smile at Roger, in which he thought he detected some real warmth, and so he smiled back in kind, or as close as he could get to it.

"I shan't be a moment," she said, "you can get undressed and get into bed if you wish." Her accent was quite good, he thought, it was a pity that she was what she was.

Roger swallowed and wished the room was not quite so well lit, no less than three lamps burned there, but he sat on the edge of the double bed, which stood behind the dressing table, and began to undress, beginning with his boots. While he undressed, he was able to observe the girl's back. Her face and shoulders were in shadow, but she could glimpse him in the mirror, he realised with some trepidation.

She stopped taking out pins and began combing out her hair. By the time she was finished, and had tied her hair back with a white ribbon, he was undressed and in bed with the covers pulled firmly up under his chin.

She stood and turned to him, still smiling. "Well, Sir Roger," she said, "it is time we became better acquainted. My name is Edith and by your choice I am your friend and companion for the night."

"How do you do," said Roger, striving to keep his voice steady.

"I do very well, thank you," she said, bantering with him. She reached up behind her back with her right hand, then brought both arms around to the front and held them down. Suddenly, the sleeves slid off her arms and the dress fell to the ground at her feet. She stepped out of it and threw it over a chair. She had not been wearing anything under her dress and now stood completely naked before him. "See what I mean?" she said, archly, looking at him straight in the eye.

Roger's mind went blank with fear when he beheld the sight. After a few seconds, a few thoughts floated into the void inside his head: her pubic hair approximated in colour to the hair on her head; she was rather heavy in the breasts and hips: she seemed very pink and white and clean and last but not least; how on earth had he been persuaded to go through with this charade?

"What do you think?" she said, smiling wickedly. "Do you like me?"

Roger, momentarily divested of the power of speech, simply nodded and hoped that she would put his silence down to being overwhelmed by her pulchritude. "Very nice," he managed at last. "Really lovely."

The girl seemed pleased and came towards him so that she stood within an arm's length of him. He had a completely insane impulse to shake her hand, but managed to suppress this at the very last second.

She got into the bed and, having tucked the covers cosily around them both, pressed herself into his arms and kissed him passionately on the lips. Her body felt very soft and warm and there seemed to be much more of her now, somehow, than his eye had measured. "I love your bristly moustache," she murmured approvingly, "do you think you could push it between my breasts?"

Roger, who was suffering from a kind of numbness, obliged her request mindlessly; whereat a slight shudder passed through her body. Soon afterwards, he had some difficulty breathing in the confined space and was obliged to withdraw.

"That was nice," she said, "but now it's time we got really started." So saying she reached down and caught hold of his still-flaccid member. "Oh! You are not ready yet. I can help you with that." Now she began to massage his manhood, at the same time kissing him and half-lying and squirming on top of him, so that her breasts rubbed against his chest.

To his surprise, because it was almost the last thing on his mind, these antics had the effect of bringing him rapidly to an erect state. She lay back with her legs apart and pulled gently at his member to signal that he should climb on top of her. He did so and she guided him into her. He began to copulate with her and was surprised to find that she did not lie still, but, rather, moved in concert with him. But then, he supposed, she was a very bad and wicked woman and this was only a further sign that she was thoroughly depraved.

Despite the fact that he was holding back for all he was worth, he suddenly climaxed. Although this had taken him by surprise, he noted that she had stopped moving just before his time of satisfaction. But then, such skills must become second nature to women of this sort, he surmised.

"Oh drat! You fetched off too soon for me," she said, when his spasms had ceased. "Never you mind, my dear, the night is still young. You must rest now and I will, too. And if you don't mind my asking, Sir Roger, is this your first time?"

Roger was still lying on top of her, with their faces only inches apart, and this increased the sense of shame which had begun with his premature climax. But, he managed to haltingly whisper: "yes."

Edith smiled broadly. "I thought as much," she said. "But

you mustn't worry, dear, everybody has a first time, even the aristos, and I should know, I've put quite a few of them on the right road in my time." She smiled again. "You must get off me, now, my dear, you're beginning to press on me, so."

Roger realised that all his tension had left him before he got off the woman; her ready acceptance of his confession had helped in that regard.

He quickly drifted off to sleep in her arms, but before he did so, he became aware that her softness and warmth had somehow merged with the softness and warmth of the bed, so that it was as if he were enclosed in a cosy animal nest of some kind where he utterly belonged; he felt as if he been there forever and wanted to stay there forever.

A little later, after what he would one day discover was the petit mort, he woke to find her gazing at him intently by candlelight, there being perceptibly less light, outside.

"Are you all right now darling?" she asked. "Are you ready for some more?"

Roger ran his mind over his body and concluded that, perhaps, he was. "Just a little, I think," he said.

The girl laughed, which discomfited him quite a lot. "Oh, I am sorry," she said, "it's just that you can't be a little ready. You either are or you aren't; that's all there is to it."

"Then I am," said Roger, a little too vehemently, perhaps, for the girl smiled broadly and almost laughed, again.

"Well let's see," she said, as she once again began to massage his soft member. She seemed pleased with the result, because she soon afterwards kissed him lingeringly and passionately. Roger felt himself respond to her and soon they were coupling with a will once again. This time he took much longer to reach his time of satisfaction and she was able to reach what seemed to be hers at least twice, some time before he did. When he climbed off her, he was still a little shocked by the fact that she clearly enjoyed the act as much or perhaps more than he did. This was a revelation to him, he had somehow gleaned the knowledge, from various male acquaintances of his, that the woman lay there like a sack of potatoes, thinking of England, and putting up with the whole thing for the sake of bearing children. He suddenly realised that Charles had never expressed such views, but then he had not expressed any to the contrary, either. Perhaps, at a later date, he might have a conversation with him to compare notes, shocking though this idea might be.

What kind of woman was Amelia; was she like Edith or was she the more conventional kind? He could not bear to consider the question; he was too terribly embarrassed that it had formed in his mind. Time, and only time, would tell. Which kind would he prefer? His mind dodged away from that question, too.

"Penny for them," asked Edith, jocularly. But he could only answer her with a smile, which covered a multitude of sins. He was rewarded by a warm smile from her, in return. He realised that he could quickly become accustomed to this kind of debauchery, if he were not very careful. As it was, he felt he had been corrupted in some way. He began to panic, but quickly calmed himself with the notion that this was a rite of passage for every man who bedded a woman for the first time. The great thing was not to give in to it.

Lucky, indeed, was the man who could talk rationally of such things with his wife. What, then, became of those men who, for whatever reason or reasons, could not?

These thoughts were rudely interrupted by a knock at the door which was swiftly followed by the entry of Charles. He was fully dressed but much dishevelled. In the corridor behind him stood Rose wearing a nightdress and holding a candelabrum which shook with agitation.

He came quickly to Roger's side of the bed and Edith covered herself demurely with a sheet. "Get up and get dressed at once," hissed Charles. "The bulldogs are at the door and they will not go away until they are satisfied there are no students here."

Oblivious to the fact that he was naked, Roger leapt out of bed and dressed as quickly as he could. As he left with Charles to join Rose, still standing outside, he flung a few sovereigns onto the bed and closed the door behind him.

He, Charles and Rose hastened down the corridor, with the candles flickering and guttering, and through a door at the end. Rose closed this behind them and held up the candelabra to reveal a windowless linen room with shelves of bed-linen rising from floor to ceiling.

"Up, up," she cried, gesturing with the candelabra.

On the verge of panic, they scrambled up the, luckily, strongly made shelves until they reached a trapdoor in the ceiling. Charles pushed it back on its hinges and they climbed up into the attic closing the trapdoor behind them. Then, in almost total darkness, they perched uncomfortably on the narrow and very dusty plank which served as a walkway over the rafters. There was a faint light from a small window at one end.

"What shall we do now?" said Roger, as soon as he had recovered his breath.

"We sit here, keeping as quiet as possible. When we hear the bulldogs arriving at the room below, we leave the attic by that window," he gestured at the small window, which didn't look large enough for a man to climb through.

"And then?" went on Roger.

"Wait and see. It will be easier to explain when we are outside," Charles replied.

"You seem to know the drill uncannily well," said Roger.

"Something of the sort happened to me once before."

"The bulldogs?"

"No, the irate former husband of one of the girls turned up with a revolver and threatened to kill every man in the place."

"You really have led a very interesting and eventful life," said Roger without a trace of irony.

"You don't know the half of it, *mon ami*," said Charles, with deep feeling.

Some time passed before they heard the voices of the bulldogs somewhere below them and Charles got up, stretched himself, and walked down the plank to the window. He opened it as silently as he could and they climbed through. Outside, they found themselves in a kind of valley between two roofs. At the far end, near some chimneys, could be seen the top of a rusty iron ladder; which proved on his reaching it to be fixed to the wall.

They climbed down this until they reached the leads of the flat roof of some sort of ground-floor extension. They were still about ten feet above the ground but, by dint of hanging down from the edge of the roof by their fingertips and then allowing themselves to fall, they reached terra firma safely.

They were just about to take to their heels, when a lad's voice shouted. "Here's somebody!" at the same time opening the shutter of a dark lantern which feebly illuminated them.

The hue and cry was quickly taken up by three more lads who must have been nearby. They quickly joined their comrade and Charles and Roger soon found themselves cornered in the right angle between a wall of the extension and a wall of the main building.

The young men all held cudgels and raised them in a threatening manner. The first lad, who seemed to be their leader, whispered something to one of the others, who then quickly departed.

He turned to Charles and Roger. "One of us has gone to fetch the bulldogs. If you stay where you are until they get here, and give us no trouble, you'll come to no harm."

This is indeed a pickle, thought Roger, his mind racing.

114

The bulldogs will be here at any moment. He glanced at Charles and was amazed to see a smile of calm assurance on his face. How could he be so calm in the face of impending utter disaster?

"Now, my friends," said Charles, addressing the assembled company as if he were in his own drawing room, calmly and somehow almost jocularly, "how would you like a gold sovereign apiece to let us go on our way?"

"No mister," said the young man with the lantern, firmly and with decision, we'm can't." The others nodded and murmured assent.

"Not even to buy your sweethearts something pretty?" This was met with silence. Roger could almost hear their minds digesting this idea, but time was running out and he fancied he could hear the footfalls of the approaching bulldogs.

"Three sovereigns each and your sweethearts will love you for ever!"

Shamefacedly, the young man with the lantern looked into the faces of his comrades. Suddenly, they all nodded as one man, Charles handed the lantern bearer a leather purse and they all stood to one side to let them pass. But, just as he and Charles moved off, one of their number spoke. "What about Jim," he demanded, raising his cudgel. He was presumably referring to the lad who had gone to fetch the bulldogs.

Charles shook him by the hand. "I think you'll find there is enough for everyone in that purse," he said, equably.

Once they had left the young men, Charles led the way down a long garden, giving a warning about an ornamental fountain, half hidden in the darkness, as they went.

They had just reached a high brick wall at the end of the garden when a tremendous altercation broke out from the house behind them. There were shouts, thuds, and the screams of the young men; clearly, the bulldogs were venting their displeasure on them, in the form of physical violence. Roger felt a great

115

deal of concern for them, but could do nothing; unless he chose to be sent down in disgrace.

"Do not worry, *mon cher*," said Charles, taking his arm, "I gave them enough to take away the pain of half a dozen such beatings."

They had some difficulty climbing over the wall and were forced to fetch a wooden bench, which they had seen on their way down the garden, rest it against the wall at an angle and use it as a kind of ladder to make good their escape into the lane which lay beyond the wall.

Roger went first. And before he jumped down from the top of the wall to join Roger in the lane, Charles dislodged the bench with a kick, so that it fell back into the garden. This was done, he explained, as they walked up the lane together, in order to throw possible pursuers off the scent. If the bench had been left leaning against the wall, it would have made the means of their escape obvious.

After reaching the Oxford road, which lay at the bottom of the lane, they managed to hail a passing carriage for hire without having to go all the way back into Thame. Soon, they were journeying home at a cracking pace; mainly because Roger had greased the driver's palm with a half-sovereign, Charles being in a financially embarrassed state.

When they got back to the university, they found that the bulldogs were out in force there, also. The proctors must have staged some sort of crackdown that evening, worse luck. But, by dint of hiding and dodging and a little ivy-climbing, they managed to regain their rooms without being apprehended.

Both men were hungry and thirsty after their adventures and they both felt badly in need of some tobacco. They repaired to Roger's rooms where his first act was to insist on paying Charles his fair share of the bounty he had given the cudgel-wielding roughs in the garden of the house in Thame. Then he produced some cold lamb, bread, butter and a bottle of wine from his provisions cupboard and both ate heartily of this simple repast before settling down with a couple of cigars in armchairs either side of the empty fireplace. Looking at the clock, Roger saw it was now past one in the morning.

"So, *mon cher*, how was your choice of girl last evening?" Charles enquired, with a wicked grin, "was she friendly or severe?"

Roger didn't really feel like discussing his encounter, but realised that it might be best to unburden himself before retiring for the night. "She was very friendly, a nice girl, very sympathetic to my personal plight."

"Did you tell her, or was it feminine instinct?" Charles was now grinning more broadly.

Roger felt discomfited, but he resolved not to show it; it was part of becoming a man, after all. "She knew," he said, softly.

"*Mon cher*, they always do. It is one of the eternal mysteries of the universe." He was more than a little sombre, now. Perhaps, he was thinking of his first time.

Roger knew that Charles' first time had involved a maidservant, because he had once said as much. The very idea had disgusted him, then, but now, after his own experience, he realised that he wanted to know more.

"What was it like for you, the first time?" said Roger.

"Ah, it was magical; it was as if a great weight had been lifted from me. But, I was very young, *mon ami*, not much more than a boy; a callow youth and I later felt the pain of love, as payment for experiencing the pleasures of the bed. "

"It was with one of your maidservants, was it not?"

"I believe you want me to go into details," said Charles, surprised. "I will make a bargain with you: I will tell you how it was for me if you will do the same about your time with your

117

girl. You agree?"

"Yes," said Roger, nodding uncertainly. "I suppose that's only fair."

"This girl was, as you say, a maidservant, she was a little older than me but not by much. She was not a virgin, whereas I was, and she knew it. She was an upstairs maid, whose tasks included bed-making, cleaning and dusting, drawing baths and so on. It was on account of her duties that I came into contact with her fairly often. But I was an innocent; even French boys have their innocence. It took me a long time to realise that I was attracted to her and even longer to discover what it was I wanted from her.

"It began when she stood a little too close to me, one day, when she was making my bed. It was a beautiful day in early summer and I had been out cycling before breakfast for the first time that year and returned rather hot and perspiring and in need of a bath and a change of clothing from my shorts and singlet. She was making my bed when I came into my bedroom and when she suddenly straightened up; she became so close to me that the hem of her skirt touched my bare leg.

"In hindsight, I believe it was my lack of proper clothing and my dishevelment which were responsible for her seeing me in a new light and which caused her ardour to be aroused." Here, he paused and looked at Roger in a quizzical way, as if for confirmation of this observation.

"Yes, yes. I have no doubt. Please go on."

Charles smiled. "Don't be so impatient, *mon cher ami*, it doesn't become you as an English gentleman."

"Don't be such an ass!"

Charles laughed. "I had better go on or soon you will die of grief. Where was I?"

Roger glared at him.

"Oh, I remember," Charles went on hastily, a result of the

118

glare, "she was standing too close to me and became aware of me in different way. I in turn, became aware of her in a different way; that is how these things proceed, *mon ami*, as if by sorcery. I had noted before this time, of course, her comeliness and sweetness, but this was different, we were now at the same level.

"Before, I had not really seen her as a person, only as someone who served my family. I can't answer for what she previously thought of me, except that she almost certainly saw me as someone as far outside her consideration as I had previously seen her as being outside mine. It was a strange feeling, *mon ami*."

"I do, at least, know something of that feeling," said Roger, "despite my lamentable inexperience in these matters."

"Good!" said Charles, smiling tolerantly. "I shall now continue my narrative, if you have no objection."

"None."

"I raised my hand and caressed her face. Even that took more courage than I really possessed at that moment. I then removed my hand and watched carefully to see what her reaction was going to be; I half expected her to strike me, report me to my father and then give notice. But those things did not happen." Charles paused for at least a minute, as if deep in thought.

"What did happen?" prompted Roger who had been unnerved by Charles' pause into thinking that his reminiscence was at an end.

"She looked deeply into my eyes, as if for guidance, and merely asked me if she should draw me a bath. I was brought back to earth by this mundane request and simply nodded my assent.

"She went to my private bathroom, which was reached by a door at the far side of my bedroom from the landing, and soon I heard water gurgling in the rudimentary plumbing which my father had but recently commissioned to be installed.

"Soon, she called out that my bath was ready and I got to the door just as she emerged. She looked me in the eye, touched my hand with hers, and whispered that I should not lock the door of the bathroom before I got in the bath, then she went out of my rooms as if to pursue her other duties."

"And then?" enquired Roger.

"I went into the bathroom, closed the door behind me, undressed and got into the bath. I should add that my mother and father were safely ensconced in the breakfast room at this time.

"I had not been very long in the bath and had just finished washing my face when I heard the sound of my bedroom door being closed and locked, and then she entered the bathroom shutting the door behind her. She smiled at me as I lay in the soapy water and when I attempted to stand up, placed her hand on my shoulder to restrain me. Then, watching me carefully the while, she removed her blouse and camisole, so that her torso and breasts were completely exposed. They were very fine. But I was rendered speechless by her actions.

She then leaned over me, took one of my hands, and placed it on one of her breasts. At the same time, she reached into the water between my legs and began to manipulate me. As she did this I pressed my wet face against her breasts and caressed them with the hand she herself had placed there. I began to think of kissing her on the mouth, but I suddenly had my climax; after which she dressed quickly and left without a word." Charles looked up with the air of someone unburdened.

"But that was not really..." Roger began.

"No, *mon cher*, assuredly it was not; but, after that, our *affaire* began in earnest. We had many, many assignations that long, hot summer, in the stable loft and other suitable trysting places, during days when she was free of her household duties."

"I see," said Roger, afterwards running his tongue over his teeth.

"Yes, *mon ami*, I sense your distaste. But you must try and remember how young I was and she not much older. That girl was my first love, she was the, how do you English put it? schoolboy crush; nevertheless, I would have given my life for her. I look back on how naïve I was with some amusement and some regret, but that is the way of naivety, yes?"

"I suppose so," said Roger. He still felt nettled, but didn't quite know why. "I had schoolboy crushes on girls too, you know, but I did not pursue them as you did."

"You should have, *mon ami*, really you should," said Charles, thoughtfully. He seemed to know why Roger was nettled.

Roger merely shook his head with some vigour.

"Do you know what became of her, *mon cher*? Charles continued, unexpectedly. "You would never guess," he went on.

Roger had largely lost interest, but he asked the obvious question. "What, then?"

"She became pregnant and had to leave the household before her condition was discovered. I gave her as much money as I could scrape together, which was more than enough to see her through her time. But I was inconsolable for months, afterwards."

"I can't say I'm surprised it ended in that way," said Roger, dryly.

"But there is a twist to this tale," said Charles, beaming. "A couple of years later, when I went to the Folies-Bergere theatre for the first time, who should be on the stage in a leading role but..."

"...Your erstwhile schoolboy crush?"

"*Exactement*! I knew that girl had hidden talents! First, she practises her arts on me, then on the whole of Paris!"

Roger made an explosive noise.

Charles laughed heartily. "And now, *mon ami*, you must tell me about your time with your girl."

Roger blinked, drank deeply from his glass, cleared his throat, and began.

The next morning, badly hung over, Roger was racked with guilt and grief about the previous evening. His grudging revelations to Charles about his experiences with his lady of the night had been the worst thing; he winced as he recalled this ordeal. Only the wine had enabled him to speak, thus.

Now, all he could think about was that he had been unfaithful to Amelia. He had somehow been carried along on a tide of deceit which had originated in his conversations with Charles. The fellow seemed to have the powers of a magician when it came to persuasion, and perhaps in all matters. He had cast a spell over him which had lasted until he awoke that morning.

He bitterly regretted his dealings with Charles and determined to avoid him until the going down ball, where he would not be able to avoid him completely. But at least he would have Amelia as his companion and dance partner for the evening. He felt a momentary pang of dreadful panic at the notion that she might, somehow, find out about his recent debauchery and abandon him forever, but he felt he could rely on Charles' discretion that far, at least; perhaps not much further, though. He was rather a dangerous person to know, mused Roger, and yet this aspect of him had not been in the least bit apparent until recently, it was a puzzle.

That evening he saw Charles at dinner, he smiled very, very engagingly at him. All that Roger could manage was a rather tight-lipped smile in return and this seemed to amuse Charles even more.

Luckily, there were still two examinations left and he would send Charles a message via his 'boy' that he would be sporting his oak in the evenings, in order to revise for them.

At length, the evening of the ball was upon him, before he could fully prepare himself; the memories of the night spent in the house in Thame still clung to his person and he could not strip them away.

As things turned out, he could never have prepared himself for the events which took place at the ball; even with a clear conscience.

To say that the whole thing was an unmitigated disaster would be a colossal understatement. To begin with, to his utter amazement, disbelief and chagrin, Charles' partner for the evening was the same young woman whom he, Roger, had bedded at the house in Thame. That this was Charles' idea of a very fine jest was made clear by the knowing looks, featuring exaggeratedly raised eyebrows, which he gave him; when nobody else could see.

Roger had fervently hoped that he would never see this particular young lady ever again, in any context or setting whatsoever, and here she was being paraded as the high-class partner of a French count. Roger allowed that she certainly looked the part, and when she was introduced by Charles to Amelia she behaved impeccably; exactly as if she were a high-born lady. As the usual niceties were being performed by all four, Roger's throat became very dry and he could almost feel the hair on the back of his neck standing up in panic lest some word or gesture betrayed the fact that he and Charles' lady were already acquainted. Happily, the moment passed and the two couples went their separate ways, for the time being at least, but worse, much worse, was soon to follow.

He had noticed that Amelia had been quite taken by Charles and he could not help noticing, as they danced, that she seemed distracted and seemed to spend a lot of time looking out across the ballroom as if she were searching for something or somebody.

Then he saw her smiling a welcoming smile and when he looked over his shoulder he saw that Charles was actually waving at her. He glared at Charles and was gratified to see that he was chastened enough to diplomatically drift away to a distant part of the floor. At least Charles had acknowledged that his behaviour, on that occasion at least, was outrageous.

Later in the evening, however, after Amelia had been away from him for an unconscionable time, he went to look for her and found her in the company of Charles; seated next to him in an anteroom and deep in conversation.

Both had been animated and their faces had been very close together and they had clearly been gazing into each other's eyes with much more intensity than was seemly. They had practically jumped apart when they observed him and Amelia had blushed deeply; knowing her as well as he did, this was a very bad sign. Charles abruptly departed with a little bow but Amelia was unable to meet Roger's eye when he asked her what, exactly, was going on.

A little later she showed great distress when he told her they were leaving and that he would escort her to her hotel.

The rift between them deepened over the next few days, when she insisted on staying on in the university town. Roger suspected she was secretly meeting Charles, although he could never discover any proof.

Then, at a meeting on her last day in Oxford, she announced that their engagement was off and, almost in the same breath, went on to tell him the dismal and unbelievable news that Charles had taken a house for the summer in a secluded part of the country, a few miles outside both the Hindthorpe and Evesham estates; that they would be travelling down there together, that afternoon; and that he would be entertaining her there, as often as it pleased him to do so, for the foreseeable future.

"Think of the scandal you will make with Charles!" he remonstrated, a little later, in her private lounge at the hotel, after she had, with obvious deep reluctance, agreed to speak to him briefly in order to clarify her earlier shocking revelations.

So brief was the meeting to be, in fact, that she had insisted that neither of them should be seated and it was conducted while both were standing at opposite sides of the room. He, at the door which led to the stairs and foyer, while she stood with her back to the bedroom door, which he could see, was furnished with a lock and key, for all the world as if she needed a bolt-hole; in the event of an attempt on his part to approach her.

"I don't care. I want to do what I want to do, for a change," she replied hotly, her body radiating defiance. "I love Charles and I mean to live with him and then marry him. Being French, he knows what romance is all about; compared to him, you are just a rather stodgy Englishman."

Roger was, for some moments, struck dumb by this criticism. The conversation had rapidly reached a point where he found himself clutching at straws, he realised. One of them was her use of the word 'rather'.

"But Amelia, Charles is a man who uses women…" He was going to add "and then discards them" but she interrupted him, an evil smile playing on her lips.

"He can use me in any way he wants, I would do anything for him; I would give my life for him."

Roger was staggered by the intensity of her avowals and the harshness in her voice. It was as if he had recently done something terrible to her and she now hated him. Recent events had caused such changes in her that he began to conceive of the idea that she had taken leave of her senses. She certainly exhibited signs of some kind of madness.

"But Amelia, think of what we have shared together over so many years. Are you going to discard all those happy memories?

Don't they mean anything to you? Anything at all?" He was unable to keep the desperation out of his voice. "Do I no longer mean anything to you?"

Amelia's expression and whole demeanour softened at this appeal and his heart was gladdened by the sight. What she said next, however, completely destroyed the effect.

"Of course I remember the happy times we had, Roger, but they are in the past, now it's time to move on and see what the future holds, instead."

"And a future with me no longer exists for you?"

"It does not," she spat.

"Please, Amelia, I beg you, with all my heart, give up this Frenchman. No good can come of an alliance between an Englishwoman and a Frenchman, even if they are both of the nobility; history has taught us that."

Amelia smiled thinly. "You are a schoolboy compared to Charles, and you are using schoolboy arguments. That shows me how your mind works."

"How does my mind work?"

"Unemotionally, like a calculating machine."

"Amelia!"

"I am sorry, Roger, but what do you think a Frenchman would do in the event an Englishman attempted to steal his fiancée?"

"I don't know."

"No, you have no idea and that's just the trouble."

Roger could have bitten off his tongue; so completely had he fallen into the trap she had set for him. "What would a Frenchman do," he enquired, lamely.

"He would kill him. Or, at the very least, he would challenge him to a duel."

"Amelia! You are so changed as to be unrecognisable, and in such a very short time! You have become bloodthirsty and bellicose!"

"Yes," she said nodding vigorously, a contemptuous smile on her lips, "it is amazing what raw, naked passion can do to a woman!"

Roger found that he was unwilling to confront the awful possibility she was speaking literally and, as a way of avoiding the subject, said. "But murder is out of the question, even if I killed Charles, today, you would despise me because I removed him from your life; leaving aside the fact that it would also be a crime."

"How do you know that I would despise you, for certain?"

"Amelia, you have entered the realm of fantasy and you are obviously beyond any reasonable or rational words I might utter."

"Prove your love for me, Roger, and there might still be a chance for us."

"How do I do that?"

"Challenge Charles to a duel and win; it is the very least you can do. If I were a nobleman I would not be able to live with myself had I not done at least that."

"But Amelia, this is 1884 not 1684. Duelling is illegal, now." He reflected he had started a lot of his protestations with 'But Amelia'.

"Pah! You cold-blooded worm! Get out of my sight. I never want to see you again."

An icy calm, from God only knew where, descended upon him, then. "Very well, Amelia, I shall do exactly as you say, I shall challenge Charles to a duel in the next several minutes."

Something of his certainty and determination must have been conveyed to her because her countenance had become chalk-white before he finished speaking. He picked up his hat, stick and gloves, and departed without a backward glance.

As he walked back to his rooms, he began to think of a possible venue for the forthcoming duel. He knew Charles would not, could not reject his challenge.

The scene faded as, with a considerable start, Roger came out of his long reverie into the present day. It was almost as if he had been asleep, dreaming a particularly memorable dream. For quite a time, afterwards, his everyday reality seemed muted, so vivid had his recollections been.

TWELVE

The following evening, after dinner, Roger sat before a good fire in the library smoking a cigar and musing, as he often did at this time of the evening, on the events of the day. Very little had occurred of note and he soon reached the end of his recollections with his little world set to rights, once more. One thing he had noticed during the day, but had paid little mind to it due to his preoccupation with other matters, was the fact that the bulkhead which had previously existed in his mind, and which had kept unpleasant memories of Charles securely behind it, especially those which involved his vile liaison with Amelia, had, since his reverie of the afternoon before, been breached, and those memories now came tumbling through his mind unhindered, like acrobats in a circus, whenever his mind was comparatively unoccupied; as now.

Memories of the hours before the duel, which had taken place at dawn the day after his ill-fated interview with Amelia, now crowded his mind whereas they had once been so painful as to be shadowy, at best.

To begin with, he remembered going back to his rooms with a face which burned with the humiliation and chagrin Amelia had heaped upon him. He sat for a few minutes to gather his composure and the notion of doing things properly suddenly came to him.

He rummaged through some drawers and cupboards before he found the object of his search. He tucked it into his jacket, before once more putting on his hat and setting off to see if Charles was in his rooms. He glanced in the mirror just before leaving and was surprised to see that his face was now drained of all colour.

"Come in," was the prompt response when he knocked at Charles' door.

Charles was sitting at his table peeling an apple with a pocket knife when Roger came into the room.

"My dear fellow!" said Charles heartily, after catching sight of him and getting to his feet in greeting. "You look as though you have just seen a ghost!"

"I have a matter of the greatest moment to discuss with you, urgently," said Roger.

"Of course, my dear fellow," said Charles, with somewhat less assurance than before. Perhaps, he had already surmised the reason for Roger's visit. "You are always welcome here, you know that," he went on, even more hesitantly. "How may I help you?"

For answer, Roger took from under his jacket the heavy, leather riding-glove he had just taken from his rooms and threw it sharply onto the floor with a loud smack, just in front of Charles' feet.

"*Comme de diable!*" Charles exclaimed in surprise, looking down at the glove. Then he looked up at Roger's set and determined face. "If this is a joke *mon ami* it is in very poor taste."

"It is no joke. I have thrown down the gauntlet, or at least the nearest equivalent to it that I possess, here at Oxford. I am challenging you to a duel." This last was for clarification, for Charles face was still blank with knitted brows. "You have duels in your country, too, do you not?"

"Yes *mon ami, mais certes!*" He was obviously still perplexed; although Roger could see light dawning in his face. "This is because of the fair Amelia, I assume. Does she know of your intention?"

"She insisted upon it," said Roger, scowling because it had

been her idea and not his.

"Ah! *Quelle méchant femme!* I am not surprised to hear it!" he said with a broad smile.

Roger was very put out at Charles' flippant way of dealing with something which was deadly serious and also, seemingly, a disparagement of Amelia. "Do you accept?" he said, sternly.

"*Certainement! Vraiment! Mon ami,*" he replied, almost cheerfully. "The Lady Amelia would assuredly have my hide, if I did not! And it is obviously much too late for apology and restitution."

"Very well then," said Roger, still nettled. "The choice of weapons, venue, date and time are yours."

"*Alors,*" said Charles after considering the matter for a minute or two, "I choose pistols at dawn, tomorrow, in the grounds of my rented house in the country, near the village of Netherholm. Bring your second with you. I shall, of course, provide mine; also I will arrange for a surgeon to be present. But I am sorry to the depths of my heart it has come to this *mon ami.*"

"I am familiar with that village," said Roger, who was grateful for the other's apology, but coldly determined to appear businesslike, "it is quite close to my estate. I shall, of course, be there a little before that time." Roger made a brisk shallow bow and turned to leave.

"Wait!" said Charles, with such urgency that at first Roger thought that he was going to call the whole thing off. Where Charles was concerned one could never be absolutely certain of anything.

"What is it?" said Roger, a little testily.

"I am sorry to ask this, *mon ami*, but I have no duelling pistols in this country and no time to buy any. You must bring with you at least three cases of such pistols and allow me to choose which pair we will use."

Roger paused. It was an unusual request, but he could fully

see, and allow for, the exigency from which it arose. "Very well, but after you have chosen the pair, my second will load my pistol and your second must do the same for you."

"I would not have it any other way *mon ami*."

Roger nodded and left without another word. But his mind was racing now and had been for the last few minutes of his time with Charles; ever since, in fact, he had uttered the word 'wait'.

When he reached his rooms, he closed the door behind him and locked and bolted it, as if to keep out the grim reaper, himself. It was surprisingly warm in his rooms and he took off his jacket before sitting down.

He sat glumly in an armchair, before the empty fireplace which his 'boy' had tastefully decorated with dark blue crepe paper that morning. His mind wandered and he found himself trivialising that he could no longer throw cigar butts into the fireplace.

With a start he came to himself with the realisation that he had not yet appointed a second and must do so at once. But who could he choose? It would have to be someone up at Oxford, as he was, because there was simply not enough time to send and receive any wires. Besides, it was a thing which had to be asked in person. The trouble was that this was the last day of term and most of his fellow students would already have left.

His first thought, oddly, was to ask Sanderson; whom he had seen in college only about twenty minutes earlier. Oddly, because Sanderson was an insensitive idiot and the very last man to appeal to for support in anything, let alone a situation like this; he would be a drain on his resources rather than a supplier of energy and good fellowship.

If he had been fighting any other man, Charles would have been his automatic choice as second. His unfailing good humour and quiet strength would have bolstered him admirably.

After considering and discarding several friends and acquaintances, he suddenly remembered Lord Robillard. He was very young, but had seemed eminently sensible and mature for his years. Also, on the few occasions they had met, they got along quite well together; save for the fact that the young peer had been very particular about the pronunciation of his name (roe-bee-yard) with the emphasis on the second syllable.

Lord Robillard had taken a small house in town for his last term; at least ten minutes' walk away from Roger's rooms. With sudden determination, he put on his hat and jacket and went out. Lord Robillard might or might not be available, but time was running out.

As he hurried through the almost deserted back streets of the town, he remembered he had heard, recently, that Lord Robillard was said to be conducting a clandestine liaison with the very pretty daughter of a bookshop proprietor. Recalling this, his steps became momentarily hesitant; but in the end he continued on his way.

Who knows? he thought, as he reached the street where Lord Robillard resided, the implications of this, if true, might even cause his lordship to delay his departure from Oxford.

As he got to within twenty feet of the address, he thought he could hear an altercation of some kind in the distance. To his surprise, although not for some reason very great surprise, the sounds of quarrelling were emanating from the very house he was seeking. Just before he knocked, he heard the unmistakable crashing sound of breaking crockery. He knocked sharply at the door, but the knock went unanswered; meanwhile the noisy debate within continued unabated. He knocked more loudly: no response.

At last, he resorted to hammering on the door so violently with his fists that the frame seemed in danger of coming away from the masonry around it; whereat the sounds of tumult ceased, abruptly.

After about a minute Roger heard the voice of Lord Robillard saying: "I really must answer the door, Veronica; it might be important, you know." In the background, and muted, Roger heard female invective in response to Lord Robillard's observation.

The door was cautiously opened and Lord Robillard's harassed pink face appeared; his hair was disarranged and his otherwise immaculate suit bore traces of a white powder; possibly flour. There was a minor contusion on his brow and a small cut on the skin over one cheekbone. "Evesham!" he exclaimed in surprise on seeing Roger. "And what can I do for you, my dear fellow?"

Before Roger could answer, Lord Robillard's face became briefly contorted with pain and a puff of breath was forced from his lips with an 'oof' as some heavy object struck him on his upper back; falling afterwards to the floor with a loud thud.

"Perhaps, I have called at an inconvenient time?" said Roger.

"Not at all, not at all, my dear Evesham. Please come in." And with that, Lord Robillard opened the door to admit him.

Roger somewhat warily entered a passage which led to the back of the small house and caught a glimpse of an attractive young woman standing at the far end. On seeing him, she ducked quickly out of sight, but Roger had time to register the fact that she was wearing night attire, that her face was red with anger or exertion and that her hair was sticking out wildly around her head like a halo.

His foot encountered something on the floor just inside the door, which, when he bent down and picked it up, turned out to be a medium-sized copy of the Bible; with old and new testaments. He offered it to Lord Robillard who received it graciously and then showed him into a room to the right of the passage which proved to be a tiny sitting room furnished with a sofa and two armchairs, set only a yard or so apart, which faced one another; all with matching coverings of bright and cheerful chintz.

The only other piece of furniture, a sideboard, stood against the wall furthest from the solitary window; which looked out onto the street.

Lord Robillard waved him into one of the armchairs and then sat in the other; afterwards balancing the Bible on one of the arms. In the distance, Roger suddenly heard a terrible scream and a shattering crash; as of a large piece of crockery being hurled onto a hard surface.

Lord Robillard winced and extended his hand. "Please forgive me," he said, "in all the excitement I forgot to greet you properly." They solemnly shook hands and then Lord Robillard sat back a little with an expectant expression on his face. "The floor is yours," he said, throwing his right hand open in Roger's direction.

"Well," said Roger, hesitatingly at first, due to the uneasy circumstances in which he found his friend, then in a rush, "I am fighting a duel at dawn tomorrow and I need a second. Are you willing to be that man?"

To his surprise, Lord Robillard's face, which had become somewhat gloomy in the last few minutes, in addition to being harassed, brightened considerably as soon as he heard Roger's request. "I cannot think of any duty I would prefer to perform; particularly at this juncture in my life. I am heartily at your service. Do you wish me to travel down with you from Oxford, today?"

"No, Robillard, I am travelling back to my estate by carriage and I cannot possibly subject you to that ordeal." Lord Robillard raised his eyebrows at this news. "Yes I know, travelling by road, particularly over fairly long distances, isn't done very much these days, but sometimes I like to do things the old-fashioned way.

It would be much better if you went by train and we met at my house, later. I will give you the address, a letter of introduction and sufficient money to cover all expenses. I might be somewhat delayed and so it would be best if you dined before I arrived. I will explain everything in the letter; so that they treat you as the honoured guest you unquestionably are. Does all that meet with your approval?"

"Eminently, Evesham, things could not be better arranged so far as I am concerned. I have a copy of Bradshaw in my study and I shall choose a convenient train and leave as soon as possible. As luck would have it, I have, this very morning, sent all my luggage on to my home by rail and all I have here can easily be accommodated in two grips which I have retained for sundries."

"Will my request cause any problems for you with your young lady?" Roger enquired. "Because if so I..."

"No, no," said Lord Robillard, hastily, with a sideways glance at the door. "I assure you it will not. Also, I have plain stationery here which you can use to compose your letter. As to money for expenses, we can come to some agreement on that when we meet at your house tonight."

Lord Robillard rose without ceremony, nodded at Roger and left the room, closing the door carefully behind him; presumably he had gone to fetch pen and paper.

A few moments passed and then came the sound, not very far away, of a woman's voice raised in anger, barely interspersed with the calm, but indistinct, voice of Lord Robillard. Then fell an ominous silence and Lord Robillard opened the door and entered with a packet bound in blue ribbon which he handed to Roger. "Here is some stationery, and here," he reached into his pocket, "is a bottle of ink and two pens." He handed them to Roger. "If you would be so good as to write the letter over there on the sideboard while I remain seated, here, I would be grateful."

It was a bit dark over at the sideboard, but Roger did not want to cause any more delay by asking for a candle or lamp. He wasn't at all sure why, but a great disquiet had descended upon him during the time his friend was out of the room, and he didn't want to stay in that house any longer than he absolutely needed to complete his task.

Once the letter was written, Roger blotted it carefully, sealed it into an envelope bearing his full address and the name of Murdoch, the under-butler, because his butler would be present during the carriage ride, and handed it to Lord Robillard with a nod. After shaking hands he then took his leave. Luckily, the young woman, Veronica, was nowhere to be seen when he left; he was glad because he neither wanted to see her nor be seen by her.

Roger walked slowly back to his rooms, he felt he needed some fresh air and exercise; in part because the house he had just left was so very clearly a troubled one. Lord Robillard had certainly got himself into some kind of scrape regarding the young woman, Veronica, that much was certain. He began to speculate that that was the reason why Lord Robillard had accepted his request with such enthusiasm and alacrity: in order to effect an honourable escape from a desperate situation.

Such thoughts were unworthy, Roger decided; Lord Robillard was an amiable and urbane man who had always seemed generous and eager to please; during the whole time he had known him at Oxford.

He arrived back at his rooms and flung himself into an armchair. He had not been sitting there for very long before the awfulness of the situation he now found himself in fell upon him like a pall.

He had never before faced a predicament like this, one where death himself, having dealt two cards with his skeletal hands, one for Charles and one for Roger, now sat waiting with infinite patience until dawn on the morrow, when they would be turned face up to reveal who had won and who had lost.

He sat at his desk, which had a view of the grassy quadrangle, outside, resplendent in the bright summer sunshine and where a few figures in gowns were to be seen going about their business of the day. Gazing at this scene, he had but one thought: I want to see many, many summers yet to come; I don't want to die by the hand of a French usurper and adulterer!

But then, he thought, this was the whole point of the duel: to punish Charles the usurper and adulterer! Some part of him wanted to kill Charles, he realised with something of a shock. The man didn't deserve to live! He, Roger, was the honourable man, the wronged man, and by God and by right he knew he should be the victor! But, as he knew only too well, as did any thinking man, that right before God was not enough to guarantee the fitting outcome: free will always came into it and free will was very unreliable.

Gradually, Roger tore his thoughts piece by piece away from the duel and its possible consequences, and, instead, turned his attention to the packing of his bags and baggage and boxes, for he, too, was leaving Oxford for his home that afternoon. He had decided, some weeks before, not to travel by train, which involved two changes; with the disagreeable prospect of moving everything from one guard's van to another each time, and had arranged for two of his carriages, together with the appropriate number of servants, to arive outside his lodgings in Oxford at three o'clock, to make the entire journey by road, instead.

It would be a tedious journey, but the method had the other advantage that at least his personal servants would be available to help him with the task of packing everything and the subsequent lifting and carrying and stowing away, all of which was considerable, because he seemed to have far more possessions in his rooms than he had brought when he came up to the university.

He had planned to have some luncheon before the carriages arrived, but realised when he thought of this, that he had no appetite. He looked at the clock, it was five minutes past two, and to save time and possible damage, he began taking his books off the shelves and stacking them in some stout wooden boxes he had bought for this purpose.

Eventually, half an hour late, he heard the sound of horses' hoofs and the rattle of wheels below his window, and on leaning out and looking down saw that his carriages had arrived.

Soon afterwards, he, together with his butler, supervised the moving of his belongings by a team of four servants, including a young lad whose usual task was that of assistant gardener. He had been chosen because he was very fit and strong.

After a nightmarish hour and a half, during which only three or four breakages occurred; luckily of things which could fairly easily be replaced, the onerous task was accomplished. Roger had one last look in all the cupboards and drawers and in all the nooks and crannies he could see, or think of, to make certain that nothing had been left behind, and then they set off for east Sussex. He hoped they would get there before nightfall, or if not, at least before midnight, because he had to rise very early the next morning and hoped to get a few hours' sleep before he did so.

He got into the second coach which was not easy because it was crammed with luggage of one sort or another, but at last he managed to squash himself in. The forward coach was slightly less full, but it also held the servants, the older ones at any rate, those who had not found a perch upon the roofs of the carriages, nor desired to do so.

Although it was very cramped in his carriage, and every bump seemed to bring him into contact with something either hard or sharp, or both, he was at least alone and he wanted, very much, to be alone; even though his thoughts tended to be so much more insistent in that case.

He resolved, after going over and over every possible permutation and combination of events which he believed could occur before, during and after the duel, to try not to think about it any more and leave it, instead, in the lap of the gods.

He looked out of the window in an attempt to distract himself and was glad that it was a pleasant, sunny and dry day. The whole thing would have had to be postponed if it had rained heavily, for fear that the carriages would have become bogged down on the unpaved roads which Jessup had carefully chosen; both because they served as short cuts and also because they avoided large towns, as far as possible, with their crowded thoroughfares and inevitable delays.

All went well for twenty miles or so and then the carriage he occupied lost a wheel, canted over onto the axle and came to a grinding halt on the hard, dry ground; there had been no rain for a week or more.

Roger got out, not without a lot of difficulty, from under some luggage which had fallen onto his head and upper body during the juddering which had occurred before the carriage came to rest. Two of the servants, including Jessup, had already climbed down from their seat and were looking at the exposed axle muttering to each other and shaking their heads; their faces bore doubtful expressions.

"Can it be mended?" enquired Roger, who was still breathing heavily after the considerable exertion of extricating himself from the luggage.

"No sir," said Jessup, after straightening up slowly, the pin's broke in two and we haven't got no spare with us. Nor anything like it," he went on as an afterthought. "The round washer's missing, too, but we'm can find that, I have no doubt." He touched his forelock.

"What can we do?" said Roger, half to himself. He heard a discreet cough beside him and turned to see that Thompson, his butler, had silently and unobtrusively appeared beside him, as if by magic.

"If I may suggest, sir, we are not far from the village of Ankleford where they have a smithy. If the lad can ride without a saddle, we can take one of the horses out of harness, for his mount, and he can take the two parts of the broken pin to the blacksmith to have it welded together, or failing that, copied. While he is gone, sir, I further suggest we have the refreshments we were going to have about ten miles further on, so that as little time as possible will be lost. We would not have to stop at that place, then, sir."

Roger, whose mind had been preoccupied with thoughts of tomorrow, had completely forgotten about both the scheduled stop and the hampers of food and drink he had requested be brought for use at that time, was cheered a little at the thought of a picnic by the side of the road. "An admirable set of suggestions, Thompson," he said. "Thank you. Please see to it that they are carried out, with one extra condition: that the blacksmith makes three pins, two copies and one welded or three copies; in case we have the same trouble again." Thompson beamed happily and gave a little bow before he went off to convey his master's instructions to the lad and the assembled company. When this had been done, everyone except the selfsame lad seemed pleased at the prospect of a break in the proceedings.

It turned out that the lad was unhappy because everyone but him would now be able to take their leisure. Roger kept him sweet by promising him he would be allowed to finish his day's work an hour earlier than usual, the next day, and that sufficient food and drink would be kept on one side for him; against his return.

Roger hoped, by this latter stratagem, to ensure he would

not tarry unduly in carrying out his errand.

Having unharnessed one of the younger horses, the boy mounted him and sat perched on his back a little unsteadily while Jessup handed him the two parts of the pin, tied up tightly in a spotted handkerchief together with more than enough small change from Roger's pocket to pay the blacksmith.

With a clicking of his tongue the lad and horse set off, taking the road described by the butler, who, it turned out, had been born very near where they now stood and as a result knew the locality very well, having roamed the adjacent lanes, villages, fields and woods as a child.

The servants got down the hampers from the roof of the first carriage and a silence fell for some time, while everyone refreshed themselves. Roger sat at a little distance from the rest, in keeping with his position in the household. His butler also sat alone, between his master and the rest of the servants who sat in a group and ate together.

The lad was gone only about half an hour and he sat and ate hungrily as soon as he had brought back the pins and some change. Roger's stratagem seemed to have worked. While he ate, Jessup and the other servants managed to lever that side of the carriage up onto a pile of stones, using a long branch, so that the wheel could be replaced; the washer having been found by Jessup a little earlier.

Soon, they were on their way, once more, and with the exception of some necessary halts, they continued on their uneventful way back to Evesham Meads; which destination they reached at ten-thirty five that evening, just as darkness was falling.

While the luggage was being taken up to Roger's rooms he made hasty enquiries of Murdoch, the under-butler, concerning Lord Robillard and learned that he had arrived, been given the Red bedroom, the one next to Roger's own bedroom, according to Roger's instructions in the letter of introduction, had dined and was now dozing in the library with some port and cigars. Thither went Roger.

"Robillard!" said Roger, when he opened the door and saw his friend. "I trust you had a good journey down?"

"Yes, everything went very well," said Robillard, a little drowsily.

"And they have looked after you well, since you arrived?"

"Couldn't ask for better treatment, Evesham. You seem to run a tight ship, here, I must say."

"Thank you," said Roger, pleased with the compliment.

"Quite a difference from the stew I was in when I last saw you."

"Oh," said Roger, uncertainly. He particularly didn't want to get into such boggy ground before the business of the duel was completed; he had more than enough food for thought on his plate, already, and didn't want any more. He would be happy to discuss Robillard's problems by the hour together, after the duel the next day. Assuming he survived the encounter, of course.

Robillard, who was perceptive, took the double hint of Roger's short answer and his harassed expression and said. "Sorry old chap. I forgot for a moment. I suppose you will be putting your affairs in order tonight and into the small hours of tomorrow in the traditional way?"

"Yes," said Roger; after deciding that Robillard was not being flippant, "I do have quite a few letters to write, including at least one to my lawyers; to be forwarded to the various parties in the event of my death. But, even before I do that, I will have to inform my poor mother of this crisis. I am afraid that I must take your leave now, so that I can see her. I won't be very long, I cannot stay with her very long at the best of times; it tires her so."

"Do whatever you have to do; I will be here for you from

this time until the duel has been fought. I am your second and I am at your service."

"Thank you. I am so very glad I chose you." With that he left Robillard and went upstairs to his mother's bedroom.

She was asleep, with the servant who nursed her keeping a candlelit vigil over her; in case she needed anything in the night. This young woman stood on seeing Roger, then curtsied and withdrew; so that he could be alone with his mother.

As luck would have it, she had been only lightly asleep and opened her eyes at the slight disturbance he had made on entering and smiled at him; so he didn't have the heartbreaking task of waking her.

"Roger!" she exclaimed joyfully, "you are back from Oxford for good?"

"Yes Mamma," said Roger, after taking her hand and kissing her cheek. "But I am afraid I have two pieces of bad news, both of which I must tell to you now."

"Cannot they wait until tomorrow, for the telling?"

"No Mamma," he said gently, "I have no choice but to tell you now. I wish it could be otherwise; but you will understand when you hear what I have to say."

"Are they something to do with Amelia?" she asked.

"Yes Mamma, they both concern Amelia." Mamma had always been as sharp as a needle, he mused, and that sharpness had not diminished with age.

"Then tell me, as quickly as you can, because you seem so very grave."

"First, I have to tell you that Amelia has broken off her engagement to me, in favour of another man."

"The hussy!" she exclaimed with surprising vigour, so that Roger was shocked. Then a silence fell between them, during which he could see her interest in some aspect or another of the situation being gradually aroused. "Is he anyone I might know?"

she enquired, at length. Her knowledge of the illustrious families of England was encyclopaedic.

"No Mamma. He is a French count."

"French!"

"Yes Mamma, I am afraid so. But that is not the worst of it. I am to fight a duel with him tomorrow at dawn; in order to avenge the insult."

Roger's mother remained silent for some time; during which the grip of her hand became perceptibly stronger.

"Oh Roger," she wailed, at last, the tears running down her face. "I have only just got you back and now you might be taken from me for ever. I cannot bear it."

"Don't worry mother," he said, "I intend to win. You know that I am a crack shot with a pistol as well as a rifle or smoothbore." He forced a certainty he did not feel into his voice and managed a confident smile; all for her benefit.

"Yes Roger that is true." she sounded a little doubtful, but at least her tears no longer flowed. She dabbed her eyes with a handkerchief. "Who is to be your second?" she enquired, having composed herself, somewhat.

Roger was encouraged by this enquiry; he felt that she must be feeling a little better about the outcome. "Lord Robillard," he answered.

"One of the Warwickshire Robillards?" she enquired.

"The very same."

"Is his name Eustace?"

"No, that is his father."

"I met Eustace once, a long time ago, at a garden party. He was a fine man."

"So is his son."

"What is his name?"

"Arthur."

"Is Arthur here now, in this house? I would so like to meet

him." She seemed quite exited by the prospect.

"Tomorrow Mamma. Arthur is resting and I have much to do this evening." Roger felt he now had to curb his mother's interest and take his leave. "In fact I must go now and begin."

"Very well Roger, but I shall not sleep a wink."

"I shall tell the nurse to give you laudanum. You must get your rest."

As Roger went back down the stairs to rejoin Robillard in the library, he wished, profoundly, that he, too, could have some laudanum that night. But it always made him feel drowsy and out of sorts the next day and he wanted above all else to have a clear head on the morrow; his life depended on it.

When he entered the library he could see that Robillard had nodded off his chair. He decided to let him sleep, for the time being. He must have been wearied by his journey. Roger was also tired, but his nerves were stretched like piano-strings and he knew he would not be able to sleep if he tried.

Since Robillard was asleep, and they were not able to converse, Roger went to the gunroom to look over the cased sets of duelling pistols. After placing half a dozen on a table and opening them he selected two pairs of flintlocks and one pair of saw-handled percussion.

All were in very good condition, one set of octagonal-barrelled flint guns particularly so. They looked as if they had not been used since being proofed. Roger decided that they would have been his choice if he had been challenged and they had been offered. They had heavy barrels and no ramrod pipes like the true duellers they were. When he held one up and sighted it in the mirror it came up to the eye beautifully; the heavy barrel would minimise the effects of recoil when the pistol was discharged. He sighed, the choice was not to be his, but if Charles chose that pair he, Roger, felt that he would be entirely happy. They spoke to him and he could tell they were his friends. As if being in his family for such a long time had made them so. Slightly ashamed, he kissed the barrels of both and willed them to be Charles' choice. Afterwards, he gave all the pistols a good rub-down with a clean rag lightly charged with gun-oil, replaced them in their cases and carried them down to the library, together with an unopened one-pound tin of Curtis and Harvey's Diamond No. 4 grain, so that Robillard could view them, in his official capacity.

Robillard was awake and was stirring up the fire, which had burned low, preparatory to adding more coals. Roger placed the cases on one of the reading tables and opened all of them so that he could appraise them. He warned him against picking any up, now that they each had a film of oil upon them.

"Why are you providing the pistols, and why three cases?" enquired Robillard.

Roger explained, citing the dearth of duelling pistols at Charles' current place of residence. The cases and the tin of powder were then placed in a cupboard so that they could be the more easily packed for the short journey to Charles' house the next morning.

The two men then occupied armchairs on opposite sides of the fire and smoked a last cigar before they went to bed. Roger announced his intention of staying up all night, since he still had several letters to write and it would hardly be worth turning in for an hour or so before rising once again. Dawn would be at about four in the morning and so they would have to set out at three, at the latest.

Roger had already alerted Jessup as to his intentions and the coachman was to have the carriage waiting at the front of the house from two-thirty until it was time to leave. Jessup, also, had announced that he would be staying up all night.

Eventually, at about half-past midnight, Robillard went upstairs to his bed. Roger promised to call him in good time.

Then he went to his study, got out pen and paper and began to write. His silent vigil was punctuated every hour by the striking of the long-case clock in the entrance hall and soon after it struck two o'clock he found he had completed his task. He sealed the letters in their envelopes, addressed them, sealed them with sealing wax, embossed them with the Evesham crest and went upstairs to call Robillard and to wash, shave and have a change of clothing.

A little later, the two friends emerged from the front door of the house into a new day where a false dawn already showed through the broken cloud-cover which moved swiftly across the sky, driven by a surprisingly chilly wind for June.

They carried the cases of pistols and some blankets which they loaded into the waiting carriage while Jessup who had wordlessly acknowledged their arrival with a short nod and a touch of his hat, had a prolonged fit of coughing so harsh it seemed to threaten the fabric of his lungs. When all was ready, Roger tapped on the glass with his cane and they set off.

Neither man had been able to eat a morsel of food before they set out although both had managed to drink a few cups of cold, black coffee which had been set on one side in the breakfast room by the kitchen staff the night before.

Just before leaving, Roger had looked himself over in the cheval glass in his dressing room and been disturbed to see how haggard and drawn his face appeared; he had hoped to present a much more debonair and dashing appearance, since Amelia would almost certainly be present. He had simply shrugged. There was no help for it now.

As the coach rattled along through the misty, eerily-lit countryside, the two men did not exchange more than three or four words apiece. Roger found himself wondering if he should have practised a little with each type of pistol the night before; but knew that that would have been cheating. All the same, he couldn't help wondering how he was going to fare. A soldier must feel like this on the morning of an important battle, he thought. He didn't care very much for the feeling, but it was all part of life's rich tapestry, he told himself. Yes, but of what use was an unfinished tapestry?

"Netherholm, sir!" shouted the coachman. Glancing out of the window Roger was just in time to see the weather-beaten wooden sign. He had given Jessup directions the night before, and it was not long before they were going up the carriage-drive to Charles' large and opulent-looking house.

As they got to within about a hundred yards, Roger and Lord Robillard looked out of the carriage windows and saw, under some tall trees in the distance, a group of people and, near them, a table with a few lanterns on it. Charles was obviously ready for them.

As they got closer, Roger could see that Amelia, wearing a hooded cloak against the morning chill, was indeed one of the assembled company. The mist had all but dispersed and there was a hint of more light just before the sun edged up above the horizon of the eastern sky.

The carriage came to rest on a curve of the drive which was only yards from the assembled group. Roger could now see that the table had been hastily fashioned from some boards placed upon two trestles.

Out of the corner of his eye, Roger also saw Amelia moving behind one of the trees, until she was quickly lost to sight. Perhaps, he thought, she had some feelings regarding this matter after all and was too ashamed to show her face until it was all over.

Robillard carried the cases of pistols to the table and shook hands with a man who stood in attendance, evidently his opposite number. The cases were arranged side-by-side upon the table by the two seconds, and all three were opened to reveal the pistols within. Charles shook hands briefly with Roger and then he appraised the pistols while Roger held his breath. After trying them for weight and handling, Charles chose the pair which Roger had hoped and prayed that he would. Roger had remained impassive during the selection process and did not show any emotion, now. In this, he was aided by the slightest trace of weariness which had begun to invade his brain just before this point and which also caused him to be a little less concerned about the duel and its gory possibilities.

The sun was a little higher in the sky and the greater available light aided the seconds as they carefully loaded the pistols with powder and shot. The case contained balls of the correct calibre; together with circular greased-leather patches to hold them tightly in the bore and the measure on the flask was set to throw the appropriate weight of powder into the barrel. The lanterns, still alight, were kept well away from the area of the table being used by the seconds during the process of loading. The pistols, once loaded, were set at half-cock and replaced in their case; so that the final choice of the pistols used could be made by Charles. Before this, Charles' second, a middle-aged man, read aloud the *Code Duello* to the assembled company in the loud, clear voice of a trained orator.

After he had finished reading, he bowed to Charles and Roger, stepped back, and then gestured to the chosen case of pistols. Charles picked one up and Roger followed suit with the other. Charles' second, accompanied by Robillard, then placed one of the lanterns on a piece of level ground and the duellists were requested to stand back-to-back near the lantern, which now served as a starting point, and, holding their pistols close to their chests, march ten paces with the seconds calling out the count, turn, and fire at will.

As Roger marched away from the lantern he was aware of a pressure in his head and a slight buzzing sound in his ears.

When the seconds called out 'ten' he turned smoothly like an automaton to behold Charles, who had already turned and pointed his pistol. As he lifted his own pistol into the line of sight along the top flat of the octagon, he saw the powder flash in the pan of Charles' pistol and the almost simultaneous bloom of white smoke from the muzzle of his gun.

He staggered as the ball from Charles' pistol grazed his right temple, but despite the blood flowing freely down his face and dripping from his chin onto the grass at his feet, he recovered his stance, and when the figure of Charles came, for the second time, squarely into his line of sight, he fired and saw him spin violently around and fall to the ground.

Before he could draw breath, a heart-rending female shriek fell upon his ears and he saw the figure of Amelia, with the hood of her cloak displaced so that she was bare-headed, rushing like someone possessed towards his fallen adversary with her wildly flapping cloak stretched out behind her.

He saw her kneel beside him and cradle his head in her arms. Unable to view the evidence of her tender concern for Charles any longer Roger turned away, just as Robillard came running up with a piece of white cloth to bind his wound.

"Are you quite all right?" asked Robillard breathlessly as he helped Roger with the bandage.

"Just a flesh wound," said Roger, more curtly than he intended. The bitterness he felt regarding Amelia had crept into his voice.

"In that case I had better go and see how the other fellow has fared," said Robillard.

"Yes," said Roger, "I would be glad to know that." Robillard knew Charles fairly well, but was avoiding the use of his name, Roger realised; probably out of a sense of loyalty.

Roger, left alone for a moment, stole a glance at Charles who was now being attended by the surgeon as well as Amelia.

Robillard, squatting on his haunches, was conversing with them.

Next, he glanced in the direction of the carriage and could see the stolid figure of Jessup sitting up on the seat and solemnly smoking a short clay, patiently waiting for the time when they would depart. Roger promised himself that it would be soon.

Robillard came back with the news that Charles had been struck in the shoulder, that the wound was not serious, and that he was just about to be carried indoors so that the ball could be removed by the surgeon.

As they stood there, Roger saw two servants removing a broad plank from the table-top. They laid the plank on the grass at Charles side, manoeuvred him onto it and used it as a make-shift stretcher to bear him away to the house. Roger could now see why the table had been fashioned by placing planks across two trestles. Amelia accompanied them without as much as a glance in his direction. Roger decided that now was as good a time as any to make their departure from this place.

As they journeyed back along the road to Evesham Meads, the sun broke through the clouds for the first time that morning; it was obviously going to be a nice day, with plenty of sunshine. Roger was not in a sunny mood, but he nevertheless planned to have a sumptuous breakfast with Robillard and his mother, if she was up; his appetite had returned with a vengeance now that he was out of danger. He would also see to it personally that Jessup had exactly the same breakfast; but taken in the servants' hall, of course.

Roger found, when he reached the house, that not only was his mother up; she was in a bath chair outside the front door, wrapped in blankets and attended by her faithful nurse. It transpired that she had given orders to be carried there, soon after the break of dawn. She was overjoyed to see Roger fit and well, but was very distressed, for a time, about the wound to his head, because, until it was cleaned and properly dressed, it looked much worse than it really was; due to the large area of congealed blood which had formed.

They sat down to eat in the sunny breakfast room and although the clouds had rolled away in the sky outside, they were still present in the mood and demeanour of Roger; he spent most of the meal brooding over his lost love and the means by which she was lost.

His mother was so cheerful about his lucky escape and so pleased to have him safely home and to be conversing with him and Lord Robillard, however, that it was infectious, and by the end of the meal he was almost restored to his usual self, except for an insuperable desire to sleep.

Lord Robillard felt the same and so as soon as they decently could, they took their leave of Roger's mother and went to their bedrooms to catch up up on their sleep. Lord Robillard promised to look in on her after dinner, to say goodbye, before he caught the evening train to Warwickshire.

After dinner, the two men retired to the smoking room to take brandy and smoke cigars. Standing in front of the fire, they talked about the events of the day and, later, the events which had prevailed when Roger first called upon Lord Robillard to ask him to be his second.

"The thing is, Evesham, the girl expected me to ask her to marry her before I went down from Oxford; that was what all that unpleasantness was about on my last day, some of which you saw when you were there. Can you imagine what my family would have thought?"

"But you did intrigue with her?"

"Yes. But I never said I'd marry her. That was some idea she got from somewhere, God knows where. It's probably the reason she chucked that Bible at me. Surely, she would have had the sense to realise matrimony was never on the cards?"

"You would have thought so, wouldn't you?" said Roger.

"You never know with women; they seem to be a law unto themselves. I never thought Amelia would turn out the way she did." Roger reflected that his problems with Amelia and Robillard's with Veronica formed a nice counterpoint to one another; if 'nice' was the appropriate word. On the one hand, you had a girl who rejected the young man to whom she had been affianced, on the other a girl who had been rejected by her young man; to whom she had certainly not been affianced.

"Damn bad show, all round," said Robillard, after taking a large draught of his brandy. "That damn girl Veronica even threatened to come up to Warwickshire to see my poor father and demand that he make me do the right thing by her! I told her I'd have the dogs set on her if she so much as showed her face! I wouldn't have, of course, you know that. But I had to say something of the sort."

"Mm, mm," said Roger, who had become lost in his own thoughts. "The trouble is that I loved her dearly," he went on.

"Who? Veronica?" Robillards's expression was very perplexed.

"No, of course not, my dear fellow, I meant Amelia. I'm afraid I am not much use to you, in these discussions just now, Robillard." As he spoke a few tears fell from his eyes.

In response to this, Lord Robillard clapped him on the back. "No use crying over spilt milk, my friend. Have some more brandy to help take away the pain."

"Yes, I know you're right." He did not quite succeed in keeping the emotion out of his voice. "I think I will have another brandy."

"That's the spirit," said Robillard. "By the way, you did call for your carriage to be at the steps by ten o' clock; to take me to the station?"

"Yes. That's all arranged." Roger looked at his watch. "In half an hour. All prepared?"

"Cases packed and standing in your hall."

"Good. How much do you think is right, for your expenses?"

"Nothin' at all, old chap. Wouldn't take a penny off you. Glad to be of service. Might need you to do the same for me one day, and all that."

"Thank you. You're very kind. Please don't hesitate to ask, at any time." Roger had temporarily fallen to using the same slightly embarrassed, clipped mode of speech of his friend. They shook hands, very firmly, smiling at each other, fondly, as they did so.

Soon, it was time for Lord Robillard to leave. Roger stood on the steps, shook him by the hand once more, wished him a safe journey and waved at the departing carriage until it was out of sight.

Then with something like reluctance he went back to the smoking room and sank heavily into an armchair. Somehow, when he was with Robillard, it hadn't occurred to either man to sit; they had both been keyed up, but for different reasons.

Roger stared at the dying fire and remembered how Amelia had screamed and run to Charles when he was injured. He had known, at that moment, that everything he and Amelia had ever had was forever lost.

Roger came out of his long reverie and into the present day. At once his present-day troubles took precedence over those of the past. He knew that he had to find the meaning of the horseshoe design and that there was only one place left in England which could possibly help him: The College of Arms in London.

THIRTEEN

Roger descended from the hansom in Queen Victoria Street just outside the College of Arms with its imposing entrance. He paid the cabbie and made his way up the steps to the doors. When he got inside he was met by a courteous, scholarly, dapper man of about sixty years of age who announced that he was the officer in waiting for that day, that his name was Geraunt Frobisher and that he was one of the heralds of the College. Roger offered him his hand and introduced himself. After he had done so the herald seemed perceptibly less starchy and formal.

"How may I be of service, Sir Roger?" asked the herald, when they were seated in his office.

For answer, Roger handed him a copy he had made of the drawing in the poetry book; larger than the original but with the same or similarly coloured inks.

The herald took the drawing and, putting on his spectacles, examined it for some time. Finally, he rose, and taking up a hand lens from his desk, went to the window where he looked at it in the better light which obtained there; he then seated himself opposite Roger, once more.

"I cannot give you an opinion until I have consulted the pictorial indices," said the herald, taking off his spectacles and blinking at Roger. "Are you in town for long?"

"Only for the day, I am afraid; but if today is inconvenient for you I can always return at a time and day which is mutually satisfactory."

Geraunt smiled, politely. "If you could come back at about

three, this afternoon, I might have something for you. Otherwise, yes, it would be necessary to call again at a later date. Please, if you would, be as punctual as you can, Sir Roger, the College closes its doors at four and we must allow time for a consultation, should it be necessary. My fee, by the way, will be five guineas whether I am successful or not."

Roger nodded and rose to his feet whereupon the herald rose to his and escorted him to the door; where they shook hands before parting.

It had been a surprisingly bright and sunny day, but now the sky was becoming rapidly obscured by fog slowly moving up from the direction of the river. On this still day, the fog threatened to become a real pea-souper, when combined with coal-smoke, and the lack of visibility would become almost total when darkness fell that evening. Roger intended to dine in town whatever the weather was doing and began looking forward to this gastric treat.

He did not hold out much hope of any advancement of the case, he realised, but this lack of faith was not due to the lack of acumen of the herald; he seemed an able and intelligent man, very deserving of his position.

Roger hailed a passing cab to take him to the Café Royal; where he once again enjoyed a leisurely luncheon; in the absence of Sanderson, once again. It was only after he was replete and enjoying a cigar that he remembered that London was supposed to be a dangerous place for him to be; he shrugged imperceptibly, there was nothing he could do about that now, in London he was and in London he would stay until he entrained for East Sussex.

He arrived at the College of Arms in plenty of time for his appointment and spent much of the time prior to it walking up and down in an area set aside for waiting. He was the only one there and so his growing agitation disturbed nobody; he was surprised at his impatience, but realised that it had arisen because he wanted to be free of the responsibility of his mission and able, once more, to turn his mind to other things. Just then, an aide sidled up to him and announced that Mr. Frobisher was ready to receive him.

He went to the office of the herald and tapped at the door, which was slightly ajar. "Please enter, Sir Roger," came from within.

He entered and the herald, who was standing behind his desk, bade him be seated and then seated himself.

"You will no doubt be pleased to know that I have solved your little conundrum," said the herald without preamble. Roger felt a slight churning in his stomach, but perhaps that was due to the rather hastily eaten meal, he had been more than usually hungry.

"Yes, I am indeed," said Roger.

"The horseshoe design was once incorporated into the arms of the now-defunct Bracklington family who once had an estate in Surrey, east of Haslemere." He paused and peered at Roger in an enquiring way.

"The family no longer exists?" prompted Roger, who was lost for any real questions.

"Not as far as we know. They fled en masse to France in November 1605 and the estate went to some distant cousins who were not entitled to use the Bracklington arms nor did they apply to us for any in their own right; before that time or since."

"Why did the family flee to France?"

"That is a very good question," the herald's voice had become noticeably more hushed, as if he was preparing Roger for some unpleasant or distasteful news. "It was believed, in November 1605, that the head of the family, Thomas Bracklington, who was a Roman Catholic, played some lesser part in the infamous

158

Gunpowder Plot. And when the conspirators were apprehended, he feared that it would only be a matter of days before he, too, would be arrested and tortured, and so he applied the only remedy available to him and his family.

"Opinion is divided as to whether he was guilty or not; some authorities state that he would indeed have been arrested had he chosen to remain in England, others believe he fled in terror for some reason completely unconnected to the Plot. Nothing has ever been proved one way or the other."

"I see," said Roger, who felt that what he had just heard was certainly food for thought. "And there is nothing left of the former estate, I take it?"

"There is the shell of a great house which was gutted by fire in 1868, but there are no longer any estate workers and the lands have largely returned to a state of desuetude."

There seemed to be no more to be said, after this, and Roger thanked the herald, gave him the fee he had nominated and took his leave.

He drifted through the streets north of the river and then across fog-bound Blackfriars Bridge, deep in thought, so much so that he sometimes collided with other pedestrians, causing them to stare at him with resentment until he had apologised and, after one particularly violent collision, given the injured party a shilling.

Eventually, he reached Waterloo and, having ascertained that there were about twenty minutes before his train departed, went into the station buffet in search of some coffee and cakes. It was very crowded in the buffet; it was close to the time when office workers and the like travelled back to the suburbs. In the event, he only stayed long enough to consume the coffee, taking the cakes in a paper bag onto his train, which, by this time, stood waiting to go out. He got into an empty first-class compartment where he could watch the bustle outside while he finished his repast in peace. By the time he had finished, and just before the train began to move, he had come to a resolution: he would go to the former Bracklington estate on the first available fine day; he would need a dry day because he would probably be out in open country for some hours.

He had business relating to the management of his own estate on the morrow and also Wednesday; if Thursday proved to be fine and dry, that would be the best day for his expedition.

FOURTEEN

Roger had spent the previous evening selecting various items he felt he would need for his expedition that day; these included field glasses, a compass, a map which had proved on inspection to be woefully out of date, but which clearly showed Bracklington Hall on the north side of a wooded valley, not far from a river which ran through it. He had also packed his revolver and a box of 24 cartridges, his official insignia from the prime minister, a folding pocket knife, a box of matches and a cigarcase with twenty cigars; and last, but not least, something for the inner man, a packet of chicken sandwiches and two bottles of light ale; this last had been added to his rucksack just before he left at eight-thirty that morning.

As he sat in the little two-carriage train, he marvelled at the fact that his journey of less than forty miles had taken almost three hours, and had involved no less than two changes at wayside stations. He was becoming hungry, despite having a larger than usual breakfast, and would have to have his packed lunch soon after making his first reconnaissance of the former Bracklington estate.

At length the train stopped at the almost deserted station which was closest to his destination; he had three miles to walk before he reached the south side of the river valley marked on the map. He gave his ticket to the collector and passed through the gate in the white picket fence. As he walked up the lane past the stationmaster's house the savoury smell of some kind of stew which featured onions reached his nostrils; the wife of the stationmaster was obviously preparing his lunch.

He realised he was more than usually preoccupied with food and mused on the possible reasons for this. After considering and rejecting several alternatives, he realised with a kind of thrill that it had its roots in the preposterous idea that he was not going to survive the expedition and that he was thinking of food a great deal because food was equated with life in his mind and he wanted to live.

He got to a crossroads which had no signposts and was obliged to stop and unpack his map. After consulting this he determined that he was on the right road and needed to continue straight on to the north until he reached a bridge, at which point the would have to leave the road and continue across country and up a fairly steep hill. Although he wanted to have his meal, now, he set himself the goal of not eating anything until he reached the top of the hill which overlooked Bracklington Hall; on the other side of the valley.

After he left the road at the place indicated by the map and began the journey up the hill, he found that the route was surprisingly difficult because of what seemed to be acres of thick bushes with thorns which were growing in such a closely packed way that there was no help for it but circumnavigate them altogether; this wasted a lot of time and did not improve his temper. That was the trouble with maps generally, he mused, as he trudged the long way around, the makers did their best to show the terrain, but nothing could really prepare the traveller for what he found on the ground.

At length, to his great relief, he discerned a small cottage or similar building ahead which seemed to have no trees beyond it, and so must stand at the hill top.

When he reached the building, which proved to be a cottage, he found that it was unoccupied and in a state of considerable disrepair; it must have been at one time the home of one of the estate workers, possibly a shepherd. On consulting the map, he found that the building was not featured, despite obviously predating its publication.

He entered the dilapidated building, which still had most of its roof and windows but whose front door was entirely missing, and climbed carefully up the debris strewn stairs to the first and only upper floor; he hoped to find an upstairs window which would afford a good view of Bracklington Hall.

In one of the bedrooms, which still contained a rusting iron bedstead, he found the window he was seeking. Having failed to open the window because it was resolutely stuck closed; he used the remnants of a curtain to wipe as much of the cobwebs and filth away from the glass of one of the panes as he could to leave a fairly clean area. He then unpacked his field glasses and used them to peer out across the valley.

The great house was still standing, but was partly obscured by a grove of tall trees. The exterior was discoloured by the fire, there were smoke smudges still visible around most of what remained of the windows and there was no longer a roof. As he gazed at the house, however, he saw, or thought he saw, a light-coloured curved structure in roughly the place where the roof used to be; but it did not extend as high above the walls as he imagined the original roof would. He kept watching and the curved structure seemed to move very slightly from side to side and back and fore; it could be a trick of the light, he thought, he would have to get closer and investigate more thoroughly. He put his field glasses back into their case and replaced them in the rucksack.

He would have to eat something before he set off across the valley, he realised; he was famished. He didn't want to have his lunch in any of the rather poky rooms of the house, so he went back downstairs and set his provisions out on a clean flat stone in an overgrown, paved area at the back, here he had a view of the valley and the advantage of being sheltered from the strong south-westerly breeze which had begun to feel cold now that the body heat which derived from his recent exertions had dissipated.

He ate his sandwiches in a surprisingly short time, afterwards drinking one of his half-pint bottles of ale. Then, he lit one of his cigars and smoked for twenty minutes or so, until the food began to get into his bloodstream. He then carefully packed all the food packaging; he didn't want to leave any traces, stood up and began to walk down the valley side towards the house. In the distance, he could see a stone bridge which traversed the river which flowed between him and the house and so he headed in that direction.

When he was about half-way to the bridge, his nostrils were assailed by a nauseating smell; it was an odour which he knew well, it took him back to his boyhood when he had performed experiments in chemistry with his father to guide him; it was the smell which was produced when iron was being dissolved in a diluted mineral acid such as sulphuric or hydrochloric to produce hydrogen. Hydrogen itself was odourless; it was the impurities in the iron which caused the formation of unpleasant-smelling by-products.

He was extremely puzzled by this smell - it was the very last thing he expected to detect in this rural environment, luckily, it waxed and waned according to the vagaries of the wind.

When he reached the overgrown road which led across the bridge, he was surprised to see several recent cart-tracks; he could tell they were recent because they had flattened new blades of grass and tufts of weeds. For the first time he began to realise that he might not be alone in the area and, accordingly, resolved to make as little noise as possible during his investigation of the house and immediate grounds.

He crossed the bridge and went up the grassy lane towards the house, as he got closer he saw that there were three or four horse-drawn vans in the area immediately in front of the steps leading up to the remains of the front door, the horses, tethered to trees, were happily pulling up and eating the coarse grass; they looked at him curiously as he went by.

Just then, he heard the sounds of hammering and sawing starting up within; he paused, listening intently. The sounds ceased after a few minutes, but their occurrence cautioned him not to approach the house via the front entrance.

Instead, he followed the curved drive until he reached a cobbled yard to the rear. Here, to his surprise, were signs of intense activity of a kind whose object he could not at first fathom; there were at least a hundred large wooden barrels which had been coated heavily with pitch. Stout rubber tubes led from the lids of these to a series of brass manifolds which in turn led to one very large manifold which culminated in a rubber pipe about four inches in diameter which passed through a wall and into the house. A steady bubbling sound emanated from these barrels, as of a gas being generated within them.

Since there seemed to be nobody about, he advanced a little further and when he caught a glimpse of a large number of empty glass carboys labelled 'Commercial Oil of Vitriol 95%' through the open doorway of a large outbuilding together with great piles of scrap iron he suddenly understood; a very large quantity of hydrogen was being generated here and was the cause of the smell he had detected earlier. He stood musing on the possible reasons for this when he heard a faint sound coming from the outbuilding which was now behind him; he half turned, in time to see the fleeting shadow of a man. The last thing he remembered was a violent blow to the back of his head.

When he recovered consciousness, he winced involuntarily as he became aware of a penetrating pain searing through his brain. At the same time his head began to swim and he felt a profound dizziness and nausea.

These indispositions made it difficult to properly apprehend his circumstances, but he had enough mental power available to him to realise that he was securely bound, hand and foot, with his arms behind him; that he was cold and stiff; and that he was on a sooty and grimy floor with his back against the wall of a dimly lit room.

When he attempted to change his position to alleviate the stiffness in his limbs he heard the distinct clinking sound of a chain and became aware that it was wrapped two or three times around his waist and was secured by a lump of metal, presumably a padlock, and fastened by some means to the wall behind him; probably the other end of the chain was fixed to a ring set into the masonry.

Through the muzziness in his eyes he could see, via a hole in the wall where a window had once been, that it had become dark outside and that the light in the room where he was being held prisoner was provided by six or seven oil lanterns which were ranged in a wide circle around something which stood on the floor about twenty feet away. This thing, whatever it was, appeared to be black and shiny with white markings of some kind on its angular sides. The vile smell, which he had noticed earlier, was very pronounced in this room.

He could hear the sounds of men talking excitedly, but was unable to pick out more than a few words here and there and so could not determine the reason for their excitement.

A sudden draught which was accompanied by a faint creaking sound from above caused him to tilt his head and look upwards, a movement which made his head swim, even more, and which almost caused him to vomit.

The talking stopped abruptly, just then, and it seemed that some kind of consensus had been reached. Soon afterwards, there came the sound of footsteps which made a crunching sound as if the man was treading on ashes or charcoal, or both. The footsteps grew louder and louder as the man approached.

"Hello, Roger," said an excruciatingly familiar voice.

With an effort, he turned his head to gaze in the direction of the speaker. To his utter amazement, the speaker proved to be Charles, holding a lantern before him. The shock of seeing his erstwhile friend, here of all places, was so great that he lost consciousness once again.

He awakened due to the stimulus of someone massaging his wrists and ankles. He was lying on some kind of mattress or palliasse with a blanket over him and the person doing the massaging was Charles. It was probably he who had released him and made him more comfortable.

This room was much smaller and cleaner and there were several other mattresses on the bare floorboards, together with piles of grimy looking blankets; the room was obviously being used as a dormitory for several people, but was now deserted save for Charles and himself. There was a powerful smell of sweat and unwashed humanity.

"So, *mon ami,* our paths cross once more, do they not," said Charles, who was sitting next to the mattress, on one of the piles of blankets.

"Yes," spluttered Roger, but I can't understand why you, of all people, are here!"

"It is a long story, *mon ami*, an interesting story, but lengthy; I am not sure you are in a fit state to hear it all, this evening."

"If I could have a little brandy and water, I might be able to stay the course. Please, by the way, do not refer to me ever again as 'my friend'; our former friendship is in smithereens." If Roger's anger was muted it was solely because of his debilitated state.

"As you wish," said Charles imperturbably, rising. "I will get you some brandy and water." He left the room taking the lantern with him so that Roger was left in the dark. Clanking sounds were heard, accompanied by splashing; a pump was clearly being used. The kitchens of the house must be nearby, mused Roger.

Charles reappeared bearing a cracked white mug, which he applied to Roger's lips, after raising his head almost tenderly. "I am sorry about the condition of the mug, but it is the only one we have which has a handle," he said. Roger drank the very cold brandy and water, and, after experiencing a slight amount of nausea, felt better. He noticed, while his head was raised, that his rucksack was at the foot of the mattress.

Charles, seated once more, must have seen this recognition in his eyes because he smiled and said: "minus your revolver and cartridges, of course. But may I offer you one of your cigars? No? Would you allow me to have one? Yes? Thank you."

"It is difficult to know where to begin," said Charles, in between puffs of smoke as he lit the cigar from the flame of the lantern.

"At the beginning is usually best," said Roger.

"Ah yes, *mon ami*. Sorry," he had seen Roger frown at this appellation. "I promise I shall not call you that any more, in fact I shall go further; I shall discard the Frenchman altogether and become an Englishman." He stood and passed his hands over his body like a conjurer performing a trick. He did seem to change in some indefinable way before resuming his seat and this change was profound in reality, because he spoke from that time on with an English accent, to Roger's intense surprise.

"You said begin at the beginning, but where is the beginning? Perhaps I should tell you, to start with, that I am a Bracklington, and as such I can justify my new English personality."

"You. A Bracklington?" expostulated Roger. "I thought you were French!"

"I am and I am not. And I am aware that you have must have heard of the Bracklingtons, or you would not be here. I

168

congratulate you on your detective work, but please do not interrupt or we will never get the whole story told. I think the best place to begin is indeed, as you have so admirably suggested, at the beginning, in November 1605."

"November 1605!"

"Please, my dear sir, let me continue. In November 1605, my distant ancestor, Thomas Bracklington, had played a minor part in the Gunpowder Plot and when the twelve conspirators were arrested, he had no desire to be the thirteenth man. He had heard terrible stories of torture being used to elicit the truth, particularly in the case of Guido Fawkes, and so he fled to France before the authorities learned of his role."

"The action of a coward," said Roger.

"Perhaps," said Charles, shaking his head slightly. "But he always swore that he would have his revenge. He did not, nor did any of his descendants; until I was born. I am going to avenge him and all the Bracklingtons."

"What do you mean by that, exactly?"

"All in good time. All in good time. Now where was I? Ah yes, my ancestor fled these islands, together with his immediate family, for the fair lands of France. He managed to bring a small fortune in gold with him and used it to buy a somewhat dilapidated chateau and vineyards and so became a vintager. This occupation was not so very different from the one he had pursued in England; he was still living off the land but that living was different in kind and, of necessity, on a much smaller scale, in the beginning, at any rate.

"Over the years, my family changed their name to one more in keeping with their new French nationality: Bracklington became Braquelin. Also over the years they overcame the derision and opposition of the native vintagers and prospered. 'Chateau Braque' as it was colloquially and commercially known became over time a perfectly acceptable white."

"I have a few bottles of it in my cellar, but I have not seen it in any wine suppliers' catalogues in the last dozen years or so," said Roger.

"That was entirely due to the Franco-Prussian war; the family lost everything and now live in comparative poverty in a ten-bedroom house on the edge of the Bois de Boulogne. My brother, who is a General and who fought in that conflict, and myself, are the last two male descendants of the original family. Between us, we hope to restore the family fortunes; indeed we hope to do rather more than just that." His face suddenly assumed a menacing expression, which was very unpleasant to witness.

"Your family certainly seems to be cursed with ill-luck," remarked Roger.

Charles face darkened with anger. "That is something of an understatement, my dear Roger," he said with a mocking laugh, "but very soon my brother and I will be in a position to lift the curse. He has the ear of the French government and it, too, seeks a reversal of bad fortune."

Roger became dimly aware of something dreadful lurking behind the other's words and felt distinctly uneasy. But he remained silent in case Charles lost patience with him and broke off his narrative; he felt an overpowering desire to know where his former friend's allusions were leading.

"Are you aware of today's date?" continued Charles, after a long silence.

"November the... ah... third?" hazarded Roger, "I'm afraid I have rather lost track of the passage of the days, lately."

"It is November the Fifth and before this day is over, I and my twelve friends will finish the task which our ancestors attempted, but which was so cruelly interrupted."

"You can't possibly mean...?"

"Yes, we are going to mine the House of Lords which has a late sitting tonight."

Roger gasped violently and then had considerable difficulty in breathing. "It is impossible," he said at last, "as every schoolboy in this country knows, the cellars under the House are regularly inspected; nothing can be concealed there without being discovered."

"Who said anything about the cellars?" said Charles with a malevolent grin, "we are going to strike from above!"

"From above? How, in the name of God? I believe you are quite insane!"

"If you knew the history of the original attempt as well as I do, you would know of a letter…"

"A letter warning of the plot," interrupted Roger. "I have heard of that letter; it mentions the fact that the parliament shall receive a terrible blow and yet not see who hurts them, or words to that effect."

"Bravo! I see you know your history, after all. You will probably also know that this was interpreted at the time as referring to a blow struck from below, from the cellars, and as a result the cache of gunpowder was discovered. So you see, there is a perverted logic in striking from above, on this occasion," said Charles with a self-satisfied smile.

"How, exactly, do you propose to carry out an attack on the House from above?" enquired Roger eyebrows raised, still incredulous.

"By using a large hydrogen balloon, of about three times the usual volume, inflated with hydrogen generated by dissolving scrap iron in 40% vitriol; made by diluting the commercial acid with water and utilising the heat thus produced to speed the process. We needed about fifteen tons of the commercial acid, in all.

"The balloon has been specially adapted to the task of lifting and accurately delivering a mine to the target; a mine containing about one ton of high-grade gunpowder. This mine will be dropped onto the roof of the debating chamber of the House from a height of approximately one hundred feet, using a special release mechanism operated by the balloonist, which will disengage it from the balloon at exactly the right moment. The mine, which is constructed of pentagonal steel plates riveted together to form a dodecahedron and sealed against inclement weather with gutta-percha at all the seams and with several coats of a solution of pitch in naphtha, applied by brush, is furnished with three triggers situated in cavities within the structure which are activated by the initial contact with the roof and which set in train three very reliable clockwork mechanisms each capable of igniting the powder by means of percussion caps and hammers after a delay of no more than thirty seconds, by which time two things will have occurred: the mine will have crashed through the roof and be on the floor of the House, and the balloon, freed of the great weight, will have very rapidly gained sufficient height to be safe from the ensuing explosion. The element of surprise will ensure that very few, if any, of the men within would have the presence of mind to flee; everyone present will be killed and the House itself will suffer almost total destruction. Does that answer your question?"

He had spoken like a savant and his description had been utterly convincing, but Roger was appalled by the calm and unemotional way Charles had spoken. In the flickering, dim light of the lantern his face had assumed a mask-like stiffness which he had never before witnessed; it was as if he had become yet another personality; one which was almost satanic in its pitilessness.

His mind was reeling, both with the revelations he had just heard and the remains of the grogginess caused by the blow to his head, and yet he knew that above all else he must remain calm and apparently unimpressed, if he was to do something, anything, to avert the impending disaster. Beyond question he

172

had to humour Charles, as one might humour a lunatic, but not to the point where he might suspect the stratagem.

Perhaps the way to get more technical information and therefore more avenues for possible sabotage was to express doubts concerning any and all aspects of the gruesome project.

"Why are you using three igniters?" enquired Roger.

"Simply because the chances of a misfire are far less likely using three instead of one."

"How are you to ensure that the balloon will arrive exactly at its intended target," enquired Roger, evenly. "Surely, it will be exposed to the vagaries of the wind which will make it impossible to steer a proper course?"

"The prevailing wind in this part of England is south-westerly, that is roughly along a line which runs from here to London and such is the case this very evening, thanks be to providence; however, a rudder is useless on a balloon, a balloon cannot be steered like a ship, so we have evolved a system of four large, multi-vaned propellers, one for each point of the compass, which are mounted laterally on the basket of the balloon and which can be turned manually to make small, but critical, right-angled adjustments to the course dictated by the wind."

"Surely a hand-cranked propeller will not provide sufficient force to have any effect on a balloon and cargo weighing two or three tons in total?"

"It is a question of little and often having the same effect as large and seldom. The balloonist, who is none other than myself," Charles gave a little bow, "will continuously observe the mariner's compass, which is fixed to the basket of the balloon. Knowing exactly what the bearing should be, relative to each landmark to be traversed *en route*, I will turn the appropriate propeller, or propellers, until the balloon comes onto that bearing; the propellers will then be used to maintain that bearing. Small corrections to the course, made over a journey of approximately forty miles, will ensure that the balloon reaches the precise destination in London," Charles smiled like a clever schoolboy smiles to a master whom he knows he has impressed.

And Roger *was* impressed; he had seldom come across such blatant, organised skulduggery before and never on such a scale. "But why are you doing this?" he asked, perplexed. "What can you possibly hope to gain? It seems to be a disproportionate amount of effort in order to achieve an act of simple revenge."

"We are not talking of a simple act of revenge," said Charles. "No, what I and my colleagues here in this house are preparing is a distraction or diversion from the really important issue. You heard, just a little while before, of my brother who is a General, the one who has the ear of the French government?"

"Yes," said Roger, cautiously.

"He has a role to play in all this, even though he remains in France; for the time being anyway. He has persuaded the French government that the time is right for an invasion of England and subsequently the rest of the British Isles."

Roger involuntarily inhaled sharply, his mind was racing, but he did not speak; he didn't want to interrupt the other's narrative at this crucial point.

Charles looked at him with some amusement and went on. "He and I began to plan this attack some years ago; but when we broached the idea to those in power in France, at the time, they were sceptical and remained so for a considerable period. However, in the fullness of time, because the plan was so very neat and so likely to succeed and because we persisted, they began to give their attention to its execution.

"My role was the simpler of the two; first, I came to England ostensibly to get an education, but in reality to trace the descendants of the men who took part in the original Gunpowder Plot, one by one, during the various vacations from Oxford and especially during the summer of this year, after graduation. The reason they were chosen was simple: they were likely to have good reason to be opposed to the Church of England and the British government.

"They were offered a chance to finish what their ancestors started, all those years ago, together with the promise of large rewards and honours from the new French regime. France is still by and large a Catholic country and that fact went a long way towards persuading them," Charles smiled in a grand manner.

"And you have those descendants here, in this building, now, today?" Roger could hardly conceal his disbelief."

"Yes, my dear Roger."

"All twelve of them?"

"No. One of them is in London. Also, two of the others are not direct descendants, but they were just as amenable as the rest when they heard my plan." Charles made a very Gallic shrug. "What does it matter?"

"And they are your loyal lieutenants?"

"They are. And they have laboured tirelessly for me and with me for the last three or four months so that the operation can be accomplished on this most momentous of days: the Fifth of November."

"I would very much like to meet them," said Roger, without thinking.

"You shall meet them, in good time," said Charles, "but, I warn you, they will not give away their present names. However, I am certain they would wish to meet a member of the ruling classes of this country. One of those whose regime is about to come to an end." This, last, was spoken portentously.

"How can you of all people say that, when you are or have been one of the ruling classes of France!"

Charles smiled his evil smile. "I am not, nor have I ever been, a nobleman; my title only exists in my imagination."

Roger's face darkened with anger and he could not prevent himself from uttering a curse: "You out-and-out blackguard!"

Charles laughed loud and long. "How I have looked forward to this time; the time when you English, whose arrogance is known throughout the world, will have to bow down to me and my kind and respect us, instead of treating us like clowns. As we speak, my dear Roger, who shall not be 'Sir' Roger for very much longer, French forces are massing on the other side of the channel and the ports are full of ships, some of them borrowed from other governments of Europe who are just as happy as France to see the fall of England after so much puffed up pride.

"The moment the House of Lords has been destroyed and the British are running around like headless chickens, our man in London who is waiting for news of that event will telegraph to my brother in France, from the day-and-night office in the Strand, the special code word which indicates the successful initiation of our venture and the first wave of the invasion fleet will be at the south coast of England before dawn." Charles spat on the floor at his feet.

"You are beyond redemption," said Roger, wearily. The weariness of his tone was intentional; he needed to draw the other out, spur him into giving away more than he really intended, so that he would try harder to impress and dismay.

"Stand up!" Charles commanded, producing a revolver from the waistband at the back of his trousers where it had hitherto been concealed by his jacket.

"Why?" said Roger, mildly.

"Because I have something to show you."

Taking up the lantern and gesturing with the revolver, which Roger could now see was his own, Charles made him stand up. He swayed and would have fallen had not Charles supported him until he got his bearings.

They made their way out of the room, Roger in the lead and Charles in the rear holding the revolver against his back with one hand and the lantern in the other so that it lit the way for both of them.

As they went down a narrow passage, Roger could discern more and more evidence of the fire which had gutted the house when he saw the smoke-blackened walls and ceiling and became aware of the odour of charred timber.

They eventually came out into the large room in which he had been confined earlier and approached the shiny, black object which he had seen at that time. It was about five feet high and, he could now see, had the names of the men involved in the original Gunpowder Plot lettered in white paint on its black and shiny panels; one name to each panel. He could only see four from where he was standing: Robert Keyes, Ambrose Rokewood, Francis Tresham and Robert Catesby. As before, the mine, for such it must be, was lit by a circle of lamps set well back on the floor around it; almost certainly they were on the floor to keep them as far away as possible from the mine and any stray hydrogen; the latter tending to rise upwards, out of harm's way. A number of stout ropes, threaded through a large ring fixed to the top, led upwards into the darkness where he could just make out the basket of the balloon.

He stood contemplating the mine, eerily lit by the lambent flames of the lamps, and was almost in awe of it. It was strange to think of the giant which slept within that hideous object; awaiting only the appropriate stimulus to burst forth and destroy all within range.

He had a momentary impulse to hurl himself against the mine, so that at least one of the triggers would be activated and the ghastly thing explode harmlessly.

His body must have twitched or otherwise betrayed something of this impulse for he heard Charles laugh shortly, before speaking. "It would need a far greater shock than that; to set it off. Consider the danger it would present if any small jolt or bump activated one of the triggers; we could never risk moving it at all.

"No, the triggers are activated by the movement of eccentric weights held in place by strong coil springs. In order for them to be displaced they require a shock at least a hundred times that which would be imparted by throwing your body against the mine with all your strength. The calculations which have been done are extensive and have been carried out by one of us, here, who has considerable skill in the fields both of engineering and mathematics; in fact, almost the entire design and construction of the mine was the responsibility of that man."

At that moment, Roger became aware that Charles' men were standing all around them, half hidden in the shadows cast by the lanterns. One in particular, a wizened little man, seemed to give a slight nod of acknowledgement as Roger's eye fell upon him. Perhaps, then, he was the engineer and mathematician to whom Charles had referred.

"At the moment," Charles continued, "the mine is acting as a partial anchor for the balloon, the rest of the lifting power is taken up with a number of sandbags attached to and contained within the basket; most of these will be jettisoned when the time is right and the balloon will then be capable of lifting the mine and the passenger." He smiled contently to himself before venturing the question which followed. "What do think of our little enterprise?"

"Your enterprise is devilish and you are all devils," observed Roger. This comment was greeted by much laughter from everyone present.

"You are tired and possibly hungry, Roger," Charles asserted, once the laughter died down, "our cuisine is very limited, I am afraid, but we have plenty of bread and butter and cheese and tea.

Rather to his surprise, Roger found himself nodding. Soon he found himself sitting at a scrubbed pine table in an untidy but reasonably clean kitchen eating cheese sandwiches prepared by Charles. It was a good thing to eat and drink something, he thought, he must keep his strength up for whatever travails the evening might bring.

"You must tell me how you found out we were here," said Charles after an interval, during which he also partook some of the sandwiches and tea. "I know, by the way, that you were retained by the prime minister, himself."

"How on earth do you know that?"

"I too, have my ways of discovering secrets."

"The simple truth is that I did not know anyone was here," said Roger. "I felt impelled to come when I discovered the origin of the horseshoe design I found in a book of poems; with the assistance of the College of Arms," said Roger.

"You found that in our encoding book?"

"Yes." Roger gave him a glance which showed he knew the true purpose of the book. "It had been drawn there, probably by the man who lived in the cottage where the book was found; the gunpowder smuggler."

"That was Ralph Thompson, a close relative of the Bracklingtons; he gave his life for our cause." His face registered a deep sorrow, and to Roger's surprise he seemed to be on the brink of tears for some moments before composing himself and continuing. "It was he who, via various French fishing boats, gradually procured all the powder for the mine; happily he had arranged delivery of all but three barrels before he was arrested."

"The powder was manufactured in the mills of Belgium, was it not?"

Charles looked startled. "You certainly know more than I gave you credit for. We would, of course, have preferred to use

179

French powder, but I was aware that the country of origin can, in some instances, be determined from the composition, and we were anxious not to provide too many clues.

"But now I must tell you that I discovered that you were on our trail weeks ago, when a curious set of circumstances arose." He paused, as if to gauge Roger's possible reaction to what he was about to say.

"Go on," said Roger, with a modicum of impatience.

"The reason I hesitated is that one factor in the set of circumstances is Amelia. She wanted to get back the letters she had written to you over the years, especially the love letters of more recent times. She knew that a request to obtain them would almost certainly be refused."

"As a matter of fact," said Roger, grimacing ruefully, "I destroyed all her letters soon after she began her liaison with you."

"I surmised as much, when they could not be found."

"What do you mean?"

"She asked me to retrieve them for her. I say asked, but actually she begged me with tears in her eyes. She knew I had great skill in the manipulation of locks of all kinds, because I had demonstrated this to her one evening; as a party piece when the conversation had languished. In fact my little demonstration gave rise to her request in the first place. She knew, or thought she knew, exactly where you kept them: locked in a bureau drawer in your library. I didn't want to violate your privacy, but she became more and more insistent, and in the end I agreed.

"We chose a dry, rather windy night, so that any small sounds I made would be masked by the sound of the wind and of course we chose a late hour so that all within your house would be asleep. In the event, it was almost four in the morning, when I successfully opened the door of the library which gave onto the terrace. I changed my leather boots for brand-new tennis shoes, so that I could move silently and so that no possible traces of footprints would be left. We knew that you would notice the letters were missing, one day, but if great care were taken you would not know exactly when they were stolen.

"I carried a small dark-lantern, one which could be adjusted so that it threw a narrow beam of light. Using it to pick my way, I went to the bureau to work on the lock of the drawer which she had specified. To my surprise, it was not locked and contained nothing but a few short lengths of blue ribbon of the kind used to tie up bundles of letters. I put one in my pocket to show Amelia, when I got back. She might, otherwise, have expressed doubts as to whether I had succeeded in my mission.

"I was just about to leave empty-handed, save for the ribbon, when I noticed a number of newspapers and the poetry book spread out over a large reading table, together with some scribbled notes. I realised, then, that you were on to us, but I also knew that you would learn very little from the personal columns because nothing which could lead anyone to us was ever included in the messages, only general references to inform our members of progress made, the dates of meetings and so forth.

"As I stood there, trying to digest the fact that you had been assigned by someone to investigate our scheme, I heard footsteps approaching the library door which led to the house."

"It was I," Roger interrupted, I couldn't sleep and came downstairs to try out an idea which had occurred to me, one which proved, in fact, to be the solution of the message code."

"I quickly retreated to the door which led to the terrace," Charles continued, "and succeeded in locking it at exactly the same time you were unlocking the other door; after which I picked up my boots, which I had left outside, and tiptoed away into the shadows. I fervently hoped that I had left no traces of my entry. I had removed one of the ribbons, but I believed that it almost certainly would not be missed."

"I never noticed it was missing," said Roger.

"Anyway, as I made my way home, I realised I had a lot of food for thought. I marvelled at the way fate had selected you, of all people, to unravel the mystery. Although I knew that you would not find our whereabouts by decoding any of the existing messages, I resolved not to use them in future to avoid the possibility of your tracing one or other of the men we used to place them, by alerting the editors of all the likely papers of what was going on, so they in turn would have the man concerned arrested, or some such stratagem; instead, I would communicate with the Brotherhood, as we had become accustomed to call our group, by ordinary post. Much more time consuming, but safer under the circumstances.

"I realised, also, that I had underestimated you as a person, I had always believed you to be something of a buffoon, but I had been completely wrong in my assessment; you were obviously someone who was intelligent and blessed with considerable reasoning power. The buffoonery must have been affected by you as some kind of disguise. As a matter of fact, it seems to be a trick much used by the English upper classes."

"I must thank you for your damning me and all the upper classes with faint praises," chuckled Roger, who had been much amused by Charles observations. "You have obviously been among French people far too long. In England it is a form of politeness to appear to be less brainy than one really is."

"*Merde!*," said Charles, completely forgetting he had recently taken a vow to revert to being an Englishman, why do you and your kind have to play such silly games."

Roger, still amused, was just about to say something which would have annoyed Charles further, but what the other said next quenched all such ideas of levity.

"Above all, I realised you were dangerous and that you would have to be eliminated. Murdered."

Roger's mind raced, once again, and he remembered the shots fired at him through the door of the shabby house in Stepney. "It was you who sent that note making the appointment in Stepney?" he shouted, outraged.

"None other. It was not I who wrote it, of course, nor was I the man behind the door of that miserable hovel, but the whole thing was my idea."

"I still don't see quite how it was managed," said Roger, who was still breathing heavily, "in particular, how did you arrange things so that you had free access to that hovel, as you call it? Did you lease it, or buy it under an assumed name?"

Charles laughed heartily. "No, my dear Roger, we most certainly did not. No man in the Brotherhood wanted to risk placing his neck in a noose. We have a motto: 'we are known by our deeds, not by our faces or names'. Signing a lease or title deed would have meant that somebody in the Brotherhood would have had to at least reveal his face and possibly some unconscious characteristic; even if a false name were used. Far too risky."

"How, then, was access accomplished?" enquired Roger, perplexed.

"By a much simpler method, one that has the merits of being thoroughly tried and tested by brigands of many different persuasions, over several centuries."

"What method?"

"We chose a seldom-frequented cul-de-sac, and then chose a house that was not too far from the entrance and not too near the public house at the far end, then three of the Brotherhood overpowered the occupants on the evening in question, after one of their number answered a knock on the door. In the event, the house proved to be occupied by an elderly man and his equally elderly wife, and her sister.

"Our men calmed them down, assured them that they would not hurt them and explained that their occupancy was going to be very short-lived; just a few hours. At most. With that, the three residents were escorted into a back room where they were bound and gagged, but otherwise made as comfortable as possible. Two of our three men then left, leaving the youngest and fittest man, a man I will call Gaston, in sole charge.

"Gaston was armed with a large calibre .450 revolver of American manufacture which had six bullets in the cylinder. He chose a lamp rather than a candle, which might have been extinguished by the muzzle blasts of the gun, and placed it so that it illuminated the inside of the door, then he drew a circle in chalk, there, at about the height and central position he judged your heart would be when you stood on the other side. When you knocked the prearranged special knock, he fired a tight group of shots straight at the circle," Charles here looked up at Roger with a rueful smile, "and then he took up the lamp and opened the door expecting to find your dead body riddled with six bullets. To his utter astonishment, there was no such body and before he had recovered his wits he saw you standing to one side with a pistol pointed at his head.

He thought he was doomed, but as you know, there was a distraction at that moment and he took the opportunity to make good his escape. His language when he reported back to me had to be heard to be believed!

"But you must tell me, my dear Roger: how did you manage to pull off such a trick? It has been the talk of the Brotherhood, including myself, ever since. Not quite the mystery of the sphinx, of course, but nonetheless remarkable."

"By means of a childhood interest in metalwork," said Roger, smiling in a way he knew was irritating. Here, after all, was his chance to reflect a little of Charles' arrogance and self-importance back at him.

"You will not say more?" Charles asked. He was obviously none the wiser, just as Roger hoped and expected, and he did not see any reason to enlighten him further. Something in Charles' subsequent entreaties, however, caused him to recount the tale of the mechanical device he had made; as a result of the little inner voice which had counselled him to be wary of knocking on the door of a total stranger in a lonely district of London in the dead of night. Charles was properly impressed and wryly congratulated him on being protected by what he called his 'guardian angel'.

After Charles had finished speaking in this mocking way, Roger's anger welled up in him once more and he had to restrain himself from rising and striking his erstwhile comrade; he knew that if he did so he would probably be dispatched with the revolver and the terrible consequences outlined by Charles for the fate of England would be realised. He told himself, once again, that he had to preserve at least an outward semblance of detachment if he were to have the smallest chance of thwarting the Brotherhood. Accordingly, he calmly asked a question to which he did not really expect an answer: "How did you discover that I had been retained by the prime minister?"

"You have a spy in your employ; but he doesn't know he is a spy," replied Charles. "I can tell you this because it no longer matters," he went on.

"Who is he?" demanded Roger, with eyes blazing, as his ire rose again; despite his resolution of a few moments ago.

"Jessup, your coachman. But as I have said, he is not aware that he has been disloyal to you. After the incident in Stepney, one of my men, on my instructions, made it his business to befriend him for a short while, but not in an obvious way. He met Jessup in the local public house where he invariably goes on the evenings of his days off. Jessup is not a man who drinks to excess, but on the other hand he never turns down the offer of a free glass of beer, or two, or three. The alcohol loosens his tongue and he has let slip one or two very important facts.

"The man who befriended him is an expert in the art of light and genial conversation and managed to discover these facts in such clever ways that Jessup probably would not recall divulging them. One of the things he let slip was that you corresponded with the prime minister; connecting this with my discovery of your work on the secret messages was a small but vital step. All we had to do, then, was have you followed whenever you went up to London and confirm that you did visit Downing Street."

"You had me followed? I saw nobody."

"No, you did not, but the man we had on your trail was eventually spotted by the police inspector who was detailed to follow you; and only just escaped his clutches."

Roger, remembering his encounter with Inspector Sullivan, nodded thoughtfully. Yet another small mystery had now been cleared up.

At this point one of the conspirators came into the room, whispered into Charles' ear and silently withdrew to the doorway, all without meeting Roger's gaze.

Charles took out his watch, a full hunter, and having pressed the crown to release the cover, consulted it, afterwards snapping it shut and replacing it in his fob pocket.

"It is almost nine and time for me to depart," said Charles. "Everything has been prepared and it only remains for me to pilot the balloon to the target."

The chill which Roger felt at the other's words was greater than anything he had hitherto felt in his life; he had been dreading this moment and did not realise fully how much, until now.

"I regret that I must, once again, tether you to that ring in the wall; it is the only one we have available." Charles, holding the revolver, requested him to stand and signalled to the man in the doorway who returned and tied Roger's hands securely behind his back while Charles kept him covered with the revolver, after which he was led back to the place where he had first regained consciousness and tethered, in a sitting position, to the ring in the wall using the chain and padlock, as before, with his feet and hands firmly bound.

"What is to be my fate?" he enquired of Charles; who made no reply before going over to the mine, which was still lit by a ring of lanterns set on the floor around it.

Roger could only assume the worst. He realised that Charles had not once asked him if anyone knew whether he intended to travel to the former Bracklington estate. Then he realised the probable reason: as things had turned out the launch of the balloon would be concluded long before anyone seriously missed him. He had to face the fact that he was not long for this world once their evil scheme reached fruition and they had time to turn their attention to his unwanted presence. He closed his eyes and felt a pang of deep despair.

A loud cheering at that moment, accompanied by whoops of delight, from the direction of the balloon made him open his eyes and look up just in time to see the mine slowly lift off the ground, while a large number of sandbags, cast over the side of the basket by Charles, thudded down onto the ground below like dead things.

Without looking in his direction, the men filed out through a doorway which had been hitherto obscured by the mine; presumably to go outside; the better to see the balloon off on its journey, leaving him completely alone.

FIFTEEN

The sight of the balloon leaving and the joyful reaction of the men to its departure renewed his resolve to escape and do something to avert the impending disaster; nervous energy flooded into his mind and body.

He felt behind him to assess the ring and its wall fixture, both were forged of substantial pieces of iron. On an impulse, he stood and braced himself against the wall so that the chain was held in as much tension as possible against the wall fastening; it did not yield even a fraction of an inch. He tried again, this time his body made almost a right-angle with respect to the wall and the muscles in his legs shuddered with the almost superhuman effort he brought to bear on the chain and its wall fixture; again there was no result.

He got down from his position and felt the ring and its wall fixture to see if anything had loosened, nothing had. But wait! The ring which had been forged from a bar of iron about an inch in diameter now had a gap in it, about a quarter of an inch wide; it clearly had not been welded at the join and this had come apart with the force to which he had subjected it.

The join must have lain to one side of a line drawn through the ring in the direction of the exerted force, so that the maximum effect had been achieved.

He now carefully arranged the ring in that alignment, once again, before pulling at the chain with all his strength. This time he actually felt the ring give way, and a few seconds after standing upright managed to pass the last link of the chain through the gap which had now been enlarged to a width of about one inch.

He was not out of the wood, yet, his hands and feet were still tied together and the chain was still secured around his waist. But he could move around, albeit with some difficulty, and he hobbled over to one of the lanterns and, opening it, used the flame to burn through the bonds at his feet.

Just as he achieved this, he heard the voices of the group of men; they were returning and were only yards away. He turned to flee, but, because his hands were still tied and could not be used to maintain his balance, stumbled against and almost fell over a ladder lying on the ground.

Roger stood stock-still, because at that moment the voices of the men grew suddenly very loud and he was convinced they had heard him. But, when they came into the room he could hear that their conversation was of subjects other than himself and he heaved a great sigh of relief.

There must have been some other reason for the increase in volume of the men's voices; probably some vagary of the architecture.

The men passed quite close to where Roger stood, but he was in shadow and they did not see him. He held his breath - he expected at least one of them to check he was still securely bound; instead, a couple of them simply took some of the lanterns as they went by and, still talking animatedly, all went down some stone steps which probably led to the cellars.

As soon as they had gone, he picked up one of the remaining lanterns using both hands and by its light crept as quietly as possible down the corridor which led to the kitchen; he had made a mental note of the route, earlier.

His first action, on reaching the kitchen, was to cut through the bonds at his wrist with the knife he had used during the meal he had eaten there. He then turned his attention to a heavily bolted door which, he hoped, led outside into the yard which contained the barrels and scrap iron and where he had been taken prisoner.

The four bolts were very stiff and as he grappled with them he expected, every second, to hear the hue and cry of the men when they discovered he was missing, but for some reason this did not happen. Perhaps, their minds were too preoccupied with the forthcoming French invasion.

At last, the door swung open, and he stepped outside with the lantern. He could see the innumerable barrels and carefully picked the best route past them before extinguishing the lantern and placing it quietly at his feet, he could not risk using it outside.

He made his way down the yard, as he did so the moon appeared from behind some thick cloud, it was only at the quarter but he was grateful for any light it might give, he needed all the help circumstances could provide for what he was to attempt next.

He had to reach a telegraph office and send a message to the only man who had the authority to muster the troops who would be needed both in the vicinity of the House of Lords; to deal with the advent of the balloon with its deadly cargo, and on the south coast of England before dawn; to repel the French invasion. The prime minister.

He made his way back down the grassy lane by which he had reached the house; at one point a loud snort gave him a considerable start, especially considering his abstracted state of mind. It was only one of the horses he had passed, earlier, whose existence he had completely forgotten. When he looked in the direction of the sound he could see by the aid of the pale moonlight that they were all lying down in the grass for the night. He mentally tried to still his pounding heart and continued on his way.

Although he knew what he would do when he reached

civilisation, he had only the haziest recollection of the way he had to go in order to get to some part of it, any part of it. The blow to his head had not served to sharpen his recall, but his disordered mind was at least capable of registering the fact that time was not on his side; in fact he roughly estimated that the balloon would arrive at its target in about two hours.

He had arrived at this figure by the use of two pieces of approximate information: one was the distance it had to travel which had been given by Charles as forty miles, the other was his countryman's rule of thumb evaluation that the speed of the wind, now blowing strongly in his face, was about twenty miles an hour.

He knew he had to do much more, in the next two hours, than telegraph the prime minister to warn him of the danger; he knew he had to get to the little station, at which he had alighted before he had begun his trek across country, and persuade the stationmaster to help him call out the local police and possibly the militia, so that they could arrest everyone at Bracklington Hall, then he must commandeer a train which would get him to London before the balloon, so that he could personally, and much more fully, appraise the Grand Old Man of the events which had transpired that evening.

As he hastened on his way back across the valley towards the ruined cottage which he could just see on the skyline by the light of the moon, he knew that he would have to use the special insignia given to him by the prime minister which, by luck or by design, he still had in his possession. He had never used it before and he fervently hoped that he would be able to convince those, with whom he would soon be negotiating, of the authority vested in the man who held it.

At last he reached the ruined cottage, but there was no time to rest now, he must continue on to the railway station and he knew that the path was beset with obstacles of all kinds including thick shrubbery and briars; he was going to look very dishevelled when he reached the stationmaster's house and that was going to be a great disadvantage when it came to getting anyone to believe what, on the face of it, sounded like the ravings of a madman.

He came down the hill, having thankfully left the thorn bushes behind him, and found there was just enough moonlight to see the bridge, below, and further on, the crossroads and the road which led to the station. He heard a train in the distance and soon could see the lights of the carriages as it moved down the valley in which Haslemere also lay; it seemed to be depressingly far off, but at least he was going in the right direction.

At length, he crossed the bridge and reached the crossroads; now the going was flat and he managed to maintain a brisk trot. His clothes were torn, his face and hands had been scratched by briars and probably streaked with dirt and he knew that he must try and find some clean water to wash them before he presented himself at the stationmaster's house.

In the darkness, he passed the house and it wasn't until he encountered the completely deserted station, lit by two or three feeble gas lamps, that he realised the fact. He rinsed his face and hands, as best he could, at a tap in the gentlemen's convenience and hurried back up the lane.

His frantic knocking at the door of the totally unlit house went unanswered for what seemed an unconscionable time until at last a stentorian, platform-trained voice informed him through the door that the last stopping train of the evening had gone through and the next wasn't due until five in the morning.

With a great deal of difficulty, Roger made the man understand that he was not enquiring about trains and at length the door was opened by a large man holding a candlestick and dressed in a nightshirt and dressing gown; he had evidently been in bed or was just about to retire for the night.

Roger tried to explain his reasons for knocking him up, but found it difficult to restrain himself from burbling incoherently; this was due to the growing urgency he felt together with the relief at finding a friendly and sympathetic ear. For some minutes this was patently not true because the man was openly hostile and suspicious. He was, however, sufficiently impressed by the insignia, after Roger showed it to him, to at least listen without interrupting. The wife, also dressed in night attire and carrying a candlestick, came into the room soon after he had finished and said, with one eye fixed on Roger, presumably in case he pounced on her: "Whatever is the matter John," to her husband. Luckily for Roger, she seemed very taken with him when he explained to her, also, who he was and what he wanted.

"We must do everything we can to help him," she said to her husband.

"I'll get dressed then, and Roger and me will go down to the telegraph room at the station," the stationmaster replied, in the manner of one who has reached a decision.

"Can we send a wire to London from there?" enquired Roger, doubtfully.

"No sir, but we can send it to Guildford and they can relay it to London," he replied. "It's lucky I saw to it the accumulators was charged today," he said over his shoulder, as he went upstairs to dress.

The telegraph room at the station was simply an alcove in the ticket office, but everything was in working order and the following wire was sent:

To: Prime Minister William Gladstone
10 Downing Street, London.

Aerial mine attack on the House of Lords using balloon

193

imminent. Clear the area immediately.

French invasion fleet due at the south coast of England nearest France before dawn. Send all available troops and ordnance to the area immediately.

Will try to reach London, via Victoria, before attack on House of Lords.

Sir Roger Evesham.

"Now," said Roger, "I need to call out the local militia and send them to the old Bracklington estate. They must surround the house, what remains of it, and arrest every man there."

"I'm a sergeant in the local militia," responded the stationmaster. A statement which gladdened Roger's heart.

"Who is the commanding officer?" enquired Roger.

"The Colonel, up at The Beeches," replied the stationmaster.

"Can I entrust you with the task of taking him my message and making sure that he calls out the men?"

"You can depend on me, sir."

"There is one more thing I must do. I must get to London with all possible speed. Any suggestions?"

"Well, sir, there is the express due through here in," he glanced at the clock, "seventeen minutes."

"The trains through here all go to Victoria, do they not?"

"Yes, sir, they do."

"Can you get it to stop and then continue to its destination?"

"I can, sir. I can even send messages down the line to keep the permanent way clear, specially, but I won't half catch it from the powers that be, sir, if I do all that."

"Don't worry about anything you do. I shall see to it that no harm comes to you. More than that, I'll make sure you are

194

rewarded, even if it has to come from my own pocket."

"Thank you, sir, but there's really no need. It's a privilege to help a man like you, sir." His hostility had completely disappeared; he had clearly been overawed by the vital importance of the telegraph message.

At that moment the telegraph repeater started clicking, and the stationmaster sat at the little desk and began transcribing. When the clicking stopped he turned and said: "It's Guildford, sir, they want to know if we really want to send that message to the prime minister, sir, or is it a joke, they want to know, sir."

"Of course, it isn't a joke. Tell them that message must be sent at all costs. Tell them that Sir Roger Evesham is with you at the time of sending. Tell them the fate of the nation depends on it."

The stationmaster bent over the telegraph key and began sending the additional message. When he had finished there was a pause of five minutes or more during which Roger could conceal his agitation no longer and paced up and down the ticket office. Then the telegraph repeater began clicking once more and the stationmaster hunched over the desk as he transcribed the short message.

"They are going to relay your message, sir," the stationmaster said. "But they say you will have to answer for the consequences."

"Thank God," breathed Roger, "I want no more than that. Now what about that express?"

For answer, the stationmaster took down about a dozen oil lamps from a shelf placed them on a bench and began to check that they were adequately supplied with fuel. Those that showed any deficiency he topped up from a large can, via a funnel.

His meticulousness irritated Roger, who was not sure what the other was doing and why and didn't want to ask, for fear of vitiating the good impression he had made, thus far.

It was only when the stationmaster began lighting them

and they burned red behind their coloured lenses that he began to grasp what they were for. He helped the stationmaster to carry them to a point about a quarter of a mile down the line from the station, where they were closely set in lines at right-angles on both sides of the tracks.

Scarcely had they finished when they heard the train in the distance, the stationmaster picked up one of the lamps and requested Roger to do likewise, then he began to wave his lamp to and fro and Roger followed suit. When the engine got within sight of the lamps, the screeching of brakes was heard and the speed of the train was much reduced, nevertheless it went a surprising distance past them before it actually came to rest and they were obliged to walk quite a way past the station before they came to the cab of the engine. By this time, several passengers were leaning out of the windows to enquire the reason for the abrupt halt.

The stationmaster and engine driver greeted each other by their first names and the stationmaster climbed up onto the footplate. Roger stayed behind on the trackbed, where he could not quite hear what was said over the hissing sound of steam escaping from the safety valve, but he could detect incredulity in the voice of the engine driver. The conference between the two men was mercifully brief and soon the stationmaster climbed back down to inform Roger that he should now get aboard the train because they would be leaving immediately. The driver had to do his best to make up for lost time. There would be some sort of enquiry by the night general manager into the reasons for the emergency halt, when they reached Victoria. Roger would have to attend and furnish a complete explanation.

As Roger climbed into the nearest carriage he fervently hoped that his interview with the general manager could be kept as short as possible, then as he somewhat wearily took a seat, the train gave a jolt and they were off non-stop for London.

The stares of the his fellow passengers were not dying down as readily as he had hoped, probably because of his tattered clothes and dirty and disordered appearance, not to mention his unusual method of boarding the train, so he got to his feet and went to one of the lavatories where he hoped to at least have a wash, smooth down his clothes as best he could, and comb his hair.

While he was doing those things, the train thundered through the night its whistle blowing frantically and more often than he was used to on expresses. He smiled at the thought that the driver was probably using the opportunity to enjoy himself as much as possible; Roger certainly did not grudge him that, providing they did not come to grief.

After he had made himself as presentable as possible he considered the idea that he ought to sit in first class, but he was afraid of getting into conversation with somebody who might recognise him as an equal and so draw him into giving a lengthy account of himself; he simply didn't feel up to doing that, so he went back to the seat he had occupied before his wash.

He rummaged through his pockets to locate his cigar case, luckily there was one remaining; his pocket knife had survived, also, and he used one of the blades to cut the end off the cigar. But he had lost his matches and had to beg a light from a young man, probably a curate, who was sitting opposite him reading a copy of the *Church Times* and smoking a curly briar.

He sat back in his seat smoking the cigar and had just begun to relax somewhat, when there was a sudden screech of brakes and the train came rapidly to a shuddering halt. The smoke turned sour in his mouth and he extinguished the cigar in a nearby ashtray. What now? He thought, despairingly. What on earth will I do if we are stuck here for hours?

He saw the guard go past the window which gave onto the corridor and got up and left the compartment determined to buttonhole him on the question of the delay. He caught up with him with no difficulty but was aware of a slight air of resignation in the guard's face when he caught his eye; Roger was aware that he had already caused a certain amount of inconvenience to the railway staff and passengers on the train, for reasons which were absolutely necessary but which were by their very nature impossible to explain and so decided to tread carefully.

"What has happened?" Roger enquired, gently.

"The fireman has had a stroke, sir," replied the guard, "and we had almost made up for the time lost since the last delay." There was a slight glint in his eye when he spoke the latter words and Roger felt a twinge of guilt.

"I am extremely sorry to hear it," said Roger, "is there anything I can do to help?"

"Nothing at all, sir. Unless you happen to be a dab hand at shovelling coal."

"How far are we from London?" enquired Roger.

"About ten miles, sir. Why do you ask?"

"Because I think that even I could shovel coal over that kind of distance. Lead me to it."

The guard's eyes bulged slightly with astonishment. "But sir," he protested, "I was only having a little joke with you about the coal shovelling. A gentleman like you oughtn't to be shovelling coal!"

"Never mind that. I've got to get to London at all costs. I have a meeting with the prime minister and have no time to waste."

"But the Railway Regulations, sir, we can't afford to go against them. They won't allow unauthorised personnel in the cab, sir, never mind work there."

"Oh, hang the Railway Regulations! I have a special warrant to proceed without let or hindrance on any journey I might make on British soil and anywhere in the Empire," Roger showed the guard his special insignia. "That should cover my working on the footplate of this engine; so that I can complete this journey. Please take me there."

The guard grumbled under his breath, but opened a nearby cupboard and took out a lamp which he lit. Then he opened one of the doors which led outside and climbed down onto the trackbed. "All right, sir, follow me."

Roger climbed down onto the trackbed and followed the guard's crunching footsteps. "By the way, how is the fireman?"

"We've took him to the guard's van, sir. He's very poorly and lying down on a bit of canvas."

"He shall soon have medical attention," declared Roger.

The guard climbed up into the cab of the engine and Roger followed. A heated argument at once began between the driver and guard about whether he should be permitted to work there, or not. In the end, the guard managed to persuade the driver to allow it; but only by speaking darkly of possible dire consequences if he did not.

The guard left and the sullen driver instructed Roger in the art of shovelling coal into the firebox. The gist of it seemed to be that he should prevent the burning coal forming thin places where the draught would make holes and slow down, or even stop, the burning of the remaining coal. He was to make sure that that did not happen and also distribute the coal evenly on the burning mass in the firebox, but without causing it to form too thick a layer, anywhere; to close the firebox doors after the fire had been satisfactorily replenished and to open them only very briefly at intervals to see that all remained well.

After this short lesson, Roger took off his jacket and hung it on a convenient out-of-the-way projection, for it was very warm in the cab, opened the firebox doors with his shovel and began stoking. Soon afterwards, to his great relief, the driver opened a valve and they got under way; Roger following his given instructions as best he could. Despite being told by the driver that it took months, if not years, to make a good fireman, it seemed to him that he managed tolerably well; he knew this because the stream of advice mingled with grumbling criticism slackened as they built up speed and, after they had covered what must have been a few miles, this gradually died away into unintelligible muttering, punctuated by occasional glances registering either incredulity and hostility.

The driver told Roger to let up on the coaling because the station was less than two miles distant and they would be standing idle for some time; until a relief fireman could be found.

As they coasted to a stop at the terminus, the driver grudgingly told Roger that his work had been "not very bad" and he accepted this great compliment with a shallow bow.

After he had donned his jacket and stepped down from the footplate, Roger became aware of a tall man in a frock coat and top hat and a smaller man in a dark suit and black bowler hat, who were coming down the platform towards him; they must be the night general manager and his assistant.

The tall man was obviously the one in authority and it was he who spoke first. "I am Graham Williams, the night general manager for this region. Are you, by any chance, Sir Roger Evesham?"

"I am Sir Roger Evesham and I am afraid that I cannot spare you very much of my time. I have to meet the prime minister and for that purpose must first determine his present whereabouts.

"Yes, Sir Roger, I was told by his office to expect you and that you would be in a hurry," said Williams. He held out his hand and Roger shook it, warmly.

"I have an envoy from the prime minister waiting for you in a carriage outside the main entrance to the station," the manager went on, " he is to escort you to the prime minister; whose present whereabouts are being kept secret. Jones, here, will take you to your carriage." The smaller man gave Roger a hopeful look.

"Good," said Roger, smiling, "I am very glad to hear it and I am glad, sir, to have made your acquaintance, but now I must leave with all possible speed." He shook hands with Williams, once more, nodded to the smaller man, who turned away and departed for the main entrance at a brisk pace; looking over his shoulder from time to time to make sure Roger was following.

Roger would have liked to have another wash, to remove coal dust, this time, before he sought the envoy, but such niceties would have to wait until after the business of the evening was complete. He noticed a clock which said ten fifty-five; he was surprised by this, it seemed that a much greater length of time had elapsed since he left the Bracklington estate.

They approached the carriage, a shiny black brougham with no identifying crest on the door; drawn by a sleek black horse. The envoy, seated inside, saw the two men through the window and hastily got out; he must have been keeping a sharp lookout for his passenger to be.

He bowed to Roger, shook his hand briefly and held the door open for him; all without speaking, he seemed very distracted. The smaller man nodded to Roger and, now that his task was completed, turned and went back into the body of the station.

The envoy rapped on the roof with his cane as soon as they were seated and the door secured, and they were off. Roger was pressed back into the cushions by the suddenness with which they moved from rest to motion; while the envoy, seated opposite, involuntarily lunged towards him from the waist, afterwards settling back again with an apologetic expression.

As they rattled through the streets at a furious pace, Roger enquired whither they were bound.

"The prime minister has chosen to use, as a centre of operations, an admiralty barge which is moored at a point approximately four hundred yards downriver from the House of Lords and on the same side," replied the envoy. "He awaits you there."

Roger was slightly taken aback by this news. It seemed to him a precarious location for a headquarters, but it was not for him to criticise the prime minister's judgement. But, before he could give any further thoughts to the situation, the carriage made a sharp turn and a few minutes later drew to a halt at the side of the river. As soon as they had come to rest, the envoy jumped up, opened the door, and then stood outside holding it open.

He got out and the envoy pointed to some steps. "The barge is moored down there, Sir Roger," he announced with a little bow, before getting back into the brougham, closing the door behind him.

With a tap on inside of the roof and a rattle of hoofs the carriage quickly vanished into the misty darkness leaving a slightly disoriented Roger on the deserted quayside.

SIXTEEN

Roger recovered himself a little and instinctively looked up the river towards the Houses of Parliament, there seemed to be a surprising amount of activity there, with numerous moving lights and several much brighter beams shining up into the sky; theatre limelights, he surmised, as he began to descend the steps.

The river was at or very near high tide, judging by the fact that he did not have to descend very far to get to the gangplank. He was just about to step onto it when a deep voice shouted: "who goes there?" and he suddenly saw that two soldiers with rifles at fixed bayonets from one of the Guards regiments were engaged in sentry-go on the deck. Seconds later, a sergeant of the same regiment came clumping up the companionway steps and appeared on deck, taking up a position between the two soldiers, he also carried a rifle with a fixed bayonet.

"Who goes there?" he repeated, at the same time changing the position of his rifle so that it pointed at Roger's heart.

"Sir Roger Evesham," declaimed Roger.

"Need proof!" said the sergeant, keeping his rifle in the same position.

Roger, realising anew that he must look a sight, fumbled in his jacket pockets, located the insignia and presented it to the sergeant who, after ordering the two soldiers to "keep 'im covered!", took it to a deck-light to see it more clearly; there was a pause of several seconds.

"Appears to be correct!" he declared, handing it back to Roger. "Stand easy!" The two soldiers came to the stand easy position. "Mister Gladstone's expecting you Sir Roger," the sergeant went on, "please go below, if you please."

"Thank you sergeant," said Roger, moving quickly to the companionway. As he went down the steps, he heard the sergeant whispering, a little too loudly, to his men: "I knew it was 'im!"

Roger reached the door at the foot of the companionway and knocked discreetly. "Enter!" shouted a voice. He opened the door and entered.

The cabin in which he found himself was lit by at least a dozen lamps and candles. Gladstone sat at a desk covered with papers and a large-scale map; his private secretary stood by his side. Roger remembered him from his visits to Number 10 and they nodded at each other. The prime minister, making notes and obviously harassed and preoccupied, did not look in his direction for some minutes.

"Sir Roger," said Gladstone when he finally looked up, "I am so very pleased that you managed to get here before the balloon went up. Or rather," he corrected himself, "before it is seen on the horizon. I would invite you to sit, but we must leave for the House of Lords at once. You must tell me as much as you can about this extraordinary turn of events as we make our way there."

Soon, a little procession was en route for the Lords; in the van were Roger and Gladstone walking side by side; behind them was the private secretary; behind him was one of the soldiers who had been on the deck of the barge; bringing up the rear was the sergeant from the same location.

Roger, now that he had the ear of the prime minister, poured his heart out volubly and with many gesticulations. Gladstone listened intently, only interrupting him when he did not understand something at the first telling or with the occasional "I see" or "I understand completely".

As they neared the House, all in the group looked up at the sky to the south west to see if there was any sign of the balloon;

there was none, and Roger, for one, wondered if some misfortune had befallen it. He did not want to think of the consequences for him if it did not put in an appearance; the wind seemed to have dropped so that it was barely perceptible, perhaps that was the reason.

As they got to the precincts of the House, Roger could see that a great crowd had gathered, dozens deep, in a rough circle around the general area; this was being kept back by policemen and soldiers from several different regiments. When Gladstone and his entourage were seen, a way was cleared for them through the cordon by a couple of police inspectors and a few army lieutenants.

When they got inside, Roger could see two large groups of soldiers armed with rifles being given instructions by two colonels assisted by a few majors.

Other soldiers, probably from the Royal Engineers, were helping to position some limelight lamps of the kind used to provide spotlights in theatres; rubber tubes, which provided the gas for them, snaked into one of the nearest doorways of the building. All the lights in both Houses had been left on and Roger enquired of the prime minister if this was wise.

"We have to leave the lights on, for the moment, so that the soldiers can have some light from the windows in which to work. I have given instructions that they be extinguished immediately the balloon is sighted. The only lights, then, will be the limelights which will be used to illuminate the balloon so that soldiers from both rifle regiments can see the target."

"You will not be using artillery of any kind?" asked Roger.

"No indeed," replied Gladstone, "the risk of shot and shell missing the target and impacting on people and buildings when it falls back to the ground is too great; small arms fire only is to be used and in that connection I would like you to meet a Mr. Edward Wetherspoon."

Gladstone signalled to a small, anxious-looking man in civilian dress who appeared to be assisting the officer in charge of the boxes of fixed ammunition. The little man acknowledged the wave and was soon standing before Roger and the prime minister.

"Mr. Wetherspoon is a scientist and inventor who has a laboratory at the arsenal at Woolwich," said Gladstone after the proper introductions had been made. "He has recently developed an idea designed to aid the use of firearms, especially the new rapid-fire guns, during the hours of darkness, which may be of crucial importance during the present crisis. I leave it to him to explain his discovery to you; he can do so far better than I."

"Well Sir Roger," said the inventor with a little bow, "the idea is a very simple one and is not really new, the only thing which is new at the present time is my approach. It is a well-known fact that a small quantity of gunpowder when lit at night produces a flash which can be seen several miles away, depending on conditions; this has long been used as a signal in warfare and for other purposes. What is less well-known is that the flash is much more visible if a little finely ground metallic magnesium is admixed with the gunpowder.

"Now, if a cylindro-conoidal lead bullet is bored into from the base, forming a narrow channel which ends near the pointed end of the bullet and this channel is then filled with a finely-ground mixture of gunpowder and magnesium powder which has been compressed during the filling using a small press, then this mixture will ignite when the bullet is fired from a gun and will, while the mixture is burning, indicate with a small flare the trajectory and point of impact. In a rapid fire gun, if one of the specially adapted bullets is used, say, in the ratio of one to every five conventional, they can be used to direct the fire more accurately to the target, at night."

"So, we will be using rapid-fire guns, tonight?" said Roger.

"No, Sir Roger, unfortunately we cannot. The special bullets are still in the experimental stage and have to be prepared by hand. At such short notice I have only been able to supply two hundred and fifty, all of which have been adapted for rifles; they will have to be used sparingly."

"So they will not be much use in directing the fire?"

"No, they will not. But their other characteristic, that of being incendiary, will be of paramount importance in causing the hydrogen of the balloon to take fire, thus bringing it down much faster; this is something conventional bullets would not achieve."

"Yes, I see that," said Roger, shaking his hand, "good man."

As the inventor went back to his ammunition case, Gladstone came back to Roger's side and spoke to him on a different topic.

"Incidentally, Sir Roger, some of the most celebrated theatres in the West End responded magnificently to our urgent request for limelights. The only, and unfortunately unavoidable, drawback was that the patrons in the various houses got wind of what was afoot, abandoned their seats, and came here with the spotlights. A great many other people followed them, which is why we have such a large crowd of spectators."

"Don't they know they are in great danger?" enquired Roger.

"Of course. But they have given their assurance that they will move away from the area when the balloon is sighted. You see that group of well-dressed men over there in the gardens?"

"Yes, I do," said Roger. "Who or what are they?"

"They are the lords who were sitting in debate this evening, together with some members of the House of Commons who by chance remained after their day's business was over. They have collectively pledged their support in the event of a fire spreading through the buildings and have vowed to do all they can to help extinguish it."

"Good," said Roger.

"I have an emergency meeting with the cabinet at midnight," said Gladstone. "I think it best that you be available, should there be any points upon which they need clarification. The main purpose of the meeting, however, is to decide how many further regiments of troops, how much more artillery and so on, we need to send to the south coast to repel the invasion. Eight regiments have already entrained for there, together with as much ordnance as possible, as a contingency. They will be in position by the early hours of tomorrow. First, however, I must collect some papers from the admiralty barge; I would be obliged if you would accompany me."

They set off through the crowd which had grown in size in the short time they had been talking. Roger reflected on the fact that the "I would be obliged" of the prime minister had in reality been a command.

He glanced up at Big Ben and saw it was now twenty five minutes to midnight; where was the balloon?

They had been back at the barge for only about ten minutes when distant gunfire and shouts and screams were heard. Gladstone, Roger and the private secretary clattered up the companionway to see whether, as they all undoubtedly believed, these sounds heralded the arrival of the balloon. They joined the three soldiers who were already gazing towards the Palace of Westminster.

They only had two pairs of field glasses between them; Gladstone peered uninterruptedly through one pair whilst the other was passed rapidly from man to man. When Roger took his turn with the glasses, he could see that the limelights were all aimed at one place in the sky, forming a cone of light. By dint of focusing the glasses at the apex of the cone, Roger could just make out the balloon, the mine, being predominantly black, was not visible at that distance; which he estimated was about half a mile. He could not swear to it, but it seemed to him that the balloon was somewhat off course; it seemed to be moving towards a point between where he stood and the Houses of Parliament. He felt a nudge at his elbow and was obliged to give the glasses to the private secretary, who lost no time in clapping them to his eyes.

Even with the naked eye it was possible to see that the balloon, still brightly illuminated by the limelights, was losing height and getting laterally closer and closer to the barge. There was another volley of shots and suddenly the balloon seemed to be illuminated from within and its outline showed much more clearly. It was only about one hundred yards away from the barge now and Roger could see that the extra illumination had come about because the balloon had been holed on the side away from him and that the escaping gas had taken fire. The fire very quickly spread, strongly illuminating the basket and the river below. He could actually see Charles in the basket struggling to climb out before the flames engulfed him.

The balloon suddenly swooped down towards the barge as the blazing hydrogen poured out more and more rapidly. As the balloon swept directly overhead Roger could see that the mine had become detached from the basket and was going to fall straight down onto the barge from a height of about eighty feet.

He heard someone shout his name in warning, turned in the direction of the sound and realised that the others had seen what he had seen and were already crossing the gangplank to the shelter of the steps. He found himself utterly alone.

Before he could make any sort of movement, the mine crashed onto the foredeck just in front of the wheelhouse, causing the nose of the barge to dip violently down; in the same moment he saw the remains of the balloon fall into the Thames about fifty feet away. The portion which remained above the water continued to burn with smoky, orange-red flames which illuminated the scene with a lurid, flickering light.

His heart leapt up into his mouth and his mind became completely blank. In a kind of daze and from some point outside his body, he saw himself walking up to the mine until he was standing next to it. Suddenly, he was back in his body and he could clearly hear the ticking of the clockwork delays.

Moving like an automaton, he picked up a nearby oar, wedged it under the lowest facet of the mine and began trying to lever it off the deck; he knew he had only seconds before the mine detonated. As he worked, he suddenly saw Amelia's face in his mind's eye, smiling at him, this in turn reminded him of how much she had once meant to him and this thought somehow kept him from fleeing; in these last seconds he no longer cared whether he lived or died.

The mine suddenly lurched to one side under the influence of his lever and teetered to within a couple of feet of the edge of the deck. Before its momentum was lost he got a purchase for his feet and shouldered against it with all his strength. Because the side of his face was now pressed against the side of the mine the ticking became supernaturally loud. Just as he formed the thought that this would be the last sound he would hear on earth, before being blasted into oblivion, the mine toppled over the side furthest from the moorings into the river and he was precipitated onto the deck. Relieved of the great weight, the nose of the barge rose and fell with a slow oscillation.

He began to crawl away from the edge of the deck and made an attempt to get to the opposite side, but before he could achieve his goal, the explosion came, lifting the front of the barge almost completely out of the water; with an accompanying colossal roar and a vast cloud of choking white smoke. The barge pitched and rocked violently but he was able to seize hold of something fixed to the deck and held on for dear life, eyes firmly closed. The water displaced by the explosion came pouring back down upon him in torrents, pieces of solid material fell on him as well; one particularly sharp piece cut into the nape of his neck causing him to scream with pain. So great was the sound of falling water that this scream was lost to the ear, like the squeak of a mouse in a thunderstorm.

At last, the noise of falling water died into silence, but as he attempted to struggle to his feet, he found that the barge was now listing to starboard; at the same time he became aware of the loud rushing and gurgling sound of water pouring into the hull via a large hole below the waterline. A few seconds later this sound abated and the barge settled in a slanting position held above the water only by the creaking mooring cables. The rotten-eggs smell of spent gunpowder was very evident.

"Are you all right?" shouted someone, suddenly, from the direction of the steps, probably the private secretary. "Yes, I am," he shouted back. "Are you all right?" he further shouted. "We are all safe and well," came the welcome answer.

With some difficulty, he climbed up the sloping deck until he got to the apex formed by deck and hull. From this vantage, he could see a group of very bedraggled figures on the steps, illuminated by the feeble gleams of a lamp held up by one of the soldiers. He was about to address a remark to the effect that he was glad they were all safe when a thin cry and a faint splash behind him in the water caused him to look in that direction. He could see a man in the water holding onto the partially-submerged edge of the deck. He knew at once it was Charles.

He shouted to the men on the steps that there was a man in the water and made his way back down the sloping deck to him. He was able to take hold of his arms and pull him out; so that his body lay on the sloping deck.

There was only the light from the remnants of the burning balloon to illuminate the injured man, despite this Roger could see that he was indeed Charles and that he was horribly burned and disfigured; evidently, his attempt to escape the flames had been a failure.

Charles made signs that he wanted to speak and Roger cradled him in his arms so that he could the better hear the faint sounds. Despite Charles' treachery, both to him personally and to the nation collectively, Roger felt nothing but pity for him at this moment.

"This is the end for me, *mon cher Roger*, and the end of everything else, *aussi*. All my schemes have come to nothing, thanks to you, but I nevertheless wish you well. *Bon chance*. Try to forgive me, if you can. But if you find you cannot, then try to forgive Amelia; she knows nothing of the Brotherhood, nor does she suspect anything." His charred lips twisted into something resembling a smile, then his eyelids fluttered and his body fell limp as his soul departed; releasing him from the agony he must have been experiencing.

Roger looked around him, dazed, and saw that the prime minister and his secretary were sitting on the sloping deck, watching him intently. He had been oblivious to everything but the dying man and had not heard their approach. They had been silent witnesses of the little drama and they were obviously perplexed as well as moved.

212

SEVENTEEN

Although the troops, together with the necessary ordnance and munitions, remained stationed on full alert along a fifty-mile stretch of the south coast of England nearest France for three months, no signs of an invading force were ever detected; their man in London, who was never captured, must have telegraphed to General Braquelin during that fateful night that the attempt on the House of Lords had been thwarted.

Even now, the following March, small groups are billeted there as observers, who took up their duties when the main force was broken up and utilised elsewhere; so that there is no possibility of a surprise attack. Telegraphic communications between the sensitive area and London have been improved so that warning messages can be quickly sent and acted upon; in the event it ever becomes necessary.

The local militia surrounded the Bracklington house and after a short battle everybody within was captured. Two who subsequently tried to flee were fatally shot while escaping. The others were all found guilty of the crime of high treason and were executed.

When Lady Amelia heard the news concerning the House of Lords, the aborted invasion and the part Charles had played; she succumbed to an attack of brain fever and was confined to her bed in Hindthorpe Hall for more than two months. When she recovered she was closely questioned by Scotland Yard about her role in the affair, but was cleared of any wrongdoing.

Roger was acclaimed as a hero and was recommended for an honour, the exact nature of which has yet to be decided. He was glad when the adulation died down and he was able to go back to his life as 'a simple country squire' as he himself termed it.

But, as he went about his duties on his estate, Roger found that he sometimes felt tearful and couldn't quite define the reasons for it. He knew that it wasn't the fact that he had lost Amelia forever, that was a closed book and he had put it fully behind him.

Curiously enough, it seemed to have something to do with the death of Charles as he lay in his arms that fateful night. Despite the fact that he had been a villain, at worst, and a rogue, at best, some part of Roger missed him. Charles had made him see certain aspects of life differently and his life had been enriched by his friendship with him.

Even the thing of which he was deeply ashamed at the time of its accomplishment, the experience he had had at the house of ill-repute in Thame, was something for which he was grateful; now that he looked at it in hindsight. Charles had been so very right about a young man 'learning the ropes' with a surrogate, before turning his attentions to the woman who was to be his wife; except there was no such woman, now.

There was one thing about Charles which he didn't understand and probably never would: his intuitive grasp of people and situations. How, for example, had he known that he, Roger, felt the beginnings of forgiveness for him, while he lay dying in his arms?

With an effort, he forced his mind back to the bills from various chandlers which lay on the desk in front of him.

That evening, after dinner, he had an overpowering desire to get out of the house despite the fact that it was pouring with rain; he would go up to the folly for an hour or so to get some fresh air.

Lady Amelia Hindthorpe, wearing only a dressing gown, sat in a recessed part of her boudoir, regarding herself in the mirror of her dressing table. The lamps which stood on either side of the mirror amply illuminated her face. She thought the illumination was too intense, but somehow she wanted to see the beginnings of the crows' feet at the corners of her eyes, the furrows of her brows, and the fine lines elsewhere in the skin of her face which, she knew, were incipient wrinkles. All these facial defects had developed in the few short months since Charles' death. The horror of that night became momentarily palpable and she shivered, despite the warmth of her bedroom.

Her parents did not have very much to do with her since her breakdown, they humoured her, but their smiles were wooden and contrived. The servants, too, looked at her askance. They curtseyed and obeyed all the proprieties, calling her milady or ma'am, but their expressions, too, were mask-like.

All these things were very hard to bear, but strangely she welcomed them and the pain which they gave her. She had done some terrible things with Charles and because of Charles and had hurt poor Roger terribly badly and must be punished.

She had, at one time, believed that one day her punishment would be complete and she would be as she once was, with everything made right again; but the days passed one by one without any sight or sign of any such improvement and she had recently begun to shed little by little any optimism she had once possessed.

She looked out of the window on the other side of the room and saw that it was getting dark. Soon, although it was raining outside and cold, indeed because it was, it would be time for her to go out on one of her evening walks in the grounds. She

215

stood up, undid the buttons at the front of her dressing gown and threw it over a chair. She stood before the mirror naked and looked at her body critically; it was still the body of a young woman, a little thinner than it had once been but still firm and unlined; it had fared much better than her face, at any rate.

Her breasts jutted proudly as they had always done, with no sign of sagging or lack of firmness. After a time, she stopped gazing at herself, dabbed her body with perfume here and there and took up a flimsy summer dress which she had laid out on the bed, earlier. It was one which had been a favourite of Roger's, when they had been sweethearts, except, unlike those earlier times, she put it on without a stitch of underclothing.

When she reached the foot of the back stairs and opened the heavy door leading to the porch, Amelia was startled to find that it was raining heavily. Some drops, driven into the porch by a squally wind, spattered her face and body. She at first felt cold, was pleased that she felt cold, and then the familiar numbness pervaded her body and mind and after that she felt no discomfort; only an overpowering sense of freedom.

She stepped from the porch into the curtain of falling rain which soaked her hair and dress in a matter of minutes. She was glad it was raining, because otherwise she would have had to make a detour to the lake shallows in order to get wet. It was very important that she was both wet and cold on her nightly rambles. She left the carriage track which ran around the back of the house, kicked off her court shoes, and set off on a short cut across the fields to the folly on the hill.

As he donned a heavy coat and waterproof, Roger momentarily paused, the lure of his comfortable study with the prospect of some vintage port and a few good cigars, consumed before a roaring fire, almost made him reconsider his decision. But he crammed his waterproof hat on his head, took up his favourite stick, and went out.

He trudged up the steep slope to the Acropolis folly with the wind whistling in his ears and the rain streaming down his face like tears. It had been a long time since he had been up here at this time of night, he mused.

He reached the entrance and went inside, it was open to the wind, but it did at least have a roof and he was glad of the shelter it gave from the rain. He sat on the stone bench which gave the best view of the hill he had just climbed and began the process of recovering his breath.

He had been seated for about five minutes when he heard a faint sound like a sigh behind him. The hairs on the back of his neck prickled and his first thought was that some tramp or traveller was lurking there in the almost total darkness. Accordingly, he rose to his feet with his stick held like a club. "Who's there?" he demanded.

Someone who had been seated on a stone bench in the shadows stood up and there was just enough light for Roger to see that it was a woman.

"Amelia?" he hazarded.

"Yes Roger, it is I," came the reply.

Roger felt a terrible anger rising up within him and was shocked at the ferocity of it; he had been certain that he would never feel any strong emotions regarding her, ever again. "What are you doing here?" he demanded. "You must know you no longer have my permission to venture onto this property."

Even as he said this, he was aware of how trite and inconsequential it sounded and how it was the sort of utterance more appropriate for a person in some petty position of authority, such as a park keeper, and felt a twinge of shame.

"I come here every evening," said Amelia in an unfamiliar sing-song voice. "After dark, when there is no one about."

"Why?" he said, swallowing the bile he felt.

"Because I am so lonely, Roger, and I want to be somewhere I remember with fondness, the better to remember someone I still love."

"You must leave at once," he commanded, without emotion. "I don't want you in my life or anywhere on my estate ever again."

"Very well, Roger. I shall leave." She began to walk towards him, since the entrance to the folly lay behind him, and he moved just outside the doorway into the still-falling rain so that she didn't get too close. As she emerged into the slightly better light which emanated from the windows of the distant house, he was amazed to see that she was barefoot and bareheaded and was wearing only a thin, sleeveless summer dress. From the leaden way the cloth moved as she walked and the draggled state of her hair he realised that she must be soaked to the skin.

"Aren't you very cold?" he asked.

"Yes Roger, I am very cold and very wet. I have been walking in the rain for hours." She smiled faintly, an act which only emphasised the impassiveness of the rest of her face.

Roger began to wonder if she had again taken leave of her senses; he knew that she had had at least one bad episode in recent months. She had stopped walking to speak to him and now seemed disinclined to move.

"Why have you done such a foolish thing?" he asked.

"Because I am so ashamed of what I did to you and I want to punish myself."

"I don't want you to punish yourself on my account," he said, almost tenderly.

"I can't help myself. I want to die, but I am too afraid of God to kill myself directly; only indirectly, by contracting pneumonia. I have walked in the cold rain many times since I recovered from my trouble."

"Amelia! I am shocked to hear you speak this way. You must know that if you kill yourself, directly or indirectly, it is the same to Him and you will have to answer to Him in either case."

Amelia began to cry, softly. "It hurts. Oh, how it hurts!"

"What does?" he asked, although he knew what she would say.

"Being alive," she wailed.

His heart hardened. "You must go now. You had better have my waterproof." He took it off and wrapped it around her shoulders. As he did this, his fingertips brushed against her icy skin. Against his will, he began to be concerned about her. He stood to one side, expectantly, and she began to walk very slowly towards the foot of the hill. He watched the familiar, slightly gawky way that she walked and felt a stabbing pain in his heart which he knew was not purely physical.

All at once, when she was about fifty yards away, her bare feet slipped on a muddy patch and she fell heavily to the ground with an audible ragged thud. He rushed to her side, as she struggled to regain her feet, and was shocked to discover, because her dress had ridden up her body in the fall and become unbuttoned at the bodice, that she wore no undergarments. If the light had been better he would have realised this earlier.

He recovered himself with an effort, silently held out his hand to take hers and helped her to her feet. This action brought their faces very close together and without warning she kissed him firmly on the lips. It was the icy cold kiss of a corpse and yet he could feel the fire that was in it; a fire which spread through his body and down to his loins.

He felt a terrible sense of shame as he pulled away from her; how could he! How could he feel the same lust towards her as

219

he had for that fallen woman in Thame?

His rational thoughts of revulsion towards her, to which he had been habituated since she abandoned him, and the response of his body towards her, now, were so disparate that he stood silently in front of her, gazing at her, completely at a loss as to what to do next. The vexation he felt about himself was so great that it would have taken very little in the way of some extra burden to make him weep.

"Roger," she said tenderly, seeing his conflict, "cannot we...?

"No, Amelia! No! We cannot!" Even as he spoke, he was not certain what it was he was refusing; the storm raging in his mind was too great.

For answer, Amelia lay down in the wet grass, for all the world as if it were a comfortable bed and, after raising the hem of her dress to her waist, held out her arms to him smiling secretively to herself the while.

Roger shuddered at this display of harlotry, which she could only have learned during her time with Charles, and felt that if he remained with her one moment longer he, too, would go insane; but he lacked the will to move. The blood began to roar in his ears and he swayed with greater and greater amplitude. An insuperable darkness invaded his vision and he felt himself fall.

He recovered consciousness to find himself lying beside Amelia in the wet grass with her arms around him; his faint could not have lasted very long. She was whispering in his ear, but her words made no sense.

Some part of him had given up the fight to keep her at bay, despite the anger he still felt towards her. Instead, memories of when he had first fallen in love with her came flooding through his mind; including the base desires he had felt at that time. He now knew he had only imperfectly repressed those desires in the years which followed.

He quickly realised that he no longer needed to repress those desires; the repression of them had become irrelevant. The fragile thing which he and Amelia had once cherished was forever shivered into atoms and nothing which occurred between them mattered any longer. He found himself embracing her and gasping with something akin to pain when he plunged his hot maleness into her icy body; it gave him pause, but he copulated with her, regardless. He was, after all, only taking something which had been promised him, something which she had so freely given to another man.

Afterwards, he must have fallen asleep; despite the fact that he had become very wet during the time he was with Amelia. He was awakened by violent shivering brought on by the cold which seemed to emanate from the earth beneath him. He raised himself on one elbow to look at Amelia, but she had gone. Only his greatcoat, which they had used as a blanket, now lay beside him.

He got stiffly to his feet and looked around, calling her name; there was no response. He went back up to the folly but that, too, was deserted; she must have gone home. The rain had stopped.

He started off down the hill from the folly, stopping only to see if he could read his watch by means of a struck match; but the matches had become damp and would not light.

He picked up his greatcoat on his way back to the house, it was heavy with moisture and streaked with mud; he would dispose of it and his other clothes on the morrow. It would never do to let his valet find them in that state.

Wearily, he drew his own bath, it was past midnight and he was desperately tired. As he lay in the warm water, he wished that he had had time to speak to Amelia at greater length; but it was of no use to wish that, he realised, she had been beyond rational discussion. At any rate, although no such arrangement had been made, he would go up to the folly tomorrow evening; he corrected himself, *this* evening, in the hope that she would do the same. There were still a lot of things he would like to hear from her lips. A true reconciliation seemed unlikely, given the strict moral climate of the times in which they lived, but perhaps some kind of arrangement might be made for her welfare; he didn't want anything bad to happen to her. He got out of the bath, dried himself less adequately than he would have liked, because he staggered about so, and collapsed into bed.

He was awakened by a thunderous knocking on his bedroom door.

"Who's that," he shouted, his heart pounding.

"Thompson sir," said the butler through the door.

"What do you want?" shouted Roger.

He heard Thompson clearing his throat. "Inspector Brown is downstairs and wishes to speak with you, sir."

"Tell him I'll come down in a few minutes."

"Very good, sir."

Roger consulted his watch and saw that it was a quarter to seven. He hurriedly pulled on a pair of trousers and slippers and exchanged his nightshirt for a conventional shirt; while he did these things he tried to imagine what the inspector wanted at this hour, but his brain was too fogged by residual drowsiness to function efficiently.

Deciding not to bother with a collar and tie, he tied a cravat around his neck, instead. Pulling on a dressing gown, he left his bedroom, tying the cord at the waist as he walked.

When he got to the foot of the main staircase, he could see, through the glass partition, the inspector, whom he had often met during his stints as a local magistrate, standing in the vestibule with his sergeant. He opened one of the glass-panelled, double doors and advanced towards the inspector with his hand outstretched. It suddenly crossed his mind that Amelia, in her unstable state, had made a rape complaint against him, but he had no time to consider the implications of this now; even if it were the case. Instead, he concentrated on keeping his face expressionless.

"How do you do, Inspector," he said, heartily, while shaking him by the hand. "How may I help you?"

"I want you to view a body, Sir Roger," responded the inspector. The sergeant nodded slightly, as if approving the inspector's choice of words.

"A body. A body?" he heard himself saying, in a surprised and shocked voice which was perfectly genuine. He was aware that both the inspector and the sergeant were carefully watching his reaction to this startling announcement.

"Yes, Sir Roger. The body of a partially clothed young woman who was found at first light by one of your estate workers, drowned in the lake known as Long Lake, near the boathouse. Lord Hindthorpe is already in attendance with Doctor Anderson, the family doctor."

"Amelia?" said Roger, incredulously.

"Yes sir, the woman has been identified as the Lady Amelia by her father, I'm afraid to say, sir."

It was on the tip of Roger's tongue to enquire, what, if anything, was he to do down at the lake, since the body had already been formally identified, but he was aware of two things: it was his lake, after all, and also he must do the bidding of the inspector without question. "I'll go upstairs and get properly dressed," he said.

"I will wait for you and we will go down to the lake together," responded the inspector.

A little later, Roger found himself trudging down to Long Lake in the company of the inspector and the sergeant, it was fine, bright early spring morning; with a little hesitant birdsong in the air. He was smoking a curly briar; partly to give himself something to do with his hands; partly because he needed the nicotine, but mainly because he had found, long ago, that he could hide behind a pipe much more effectively than a cigar or a cigarette and he felt the need to conceal himself as much as he could that morning.

When they reached the corner of the lane from which the boathouse could be seen, Roger could see that a sail from one of the skiffs had been laid out on the little landing stage, and that three men were standing near it. The sail had some large object concealed beneath it and Roger found that he had to apply a little more mental effort just to keep walking at the same pace.

Roger greeted and shook hands with a grim-faced Lord Hindthorpe and an almost equally grim-faced Doctor Anderson whom he knew slightly. He nodded at the other man, dressed in rough clothes, who must be the estate worker who found the body. He looked familiar to Roger, but he could not put a name to the face.

The sail was moved to one side and the ghastly white body of Amelia was revealed, lying face-upwards in her summer dress. She seemed smaller than he remembered her, somehow, despite being puffy with water absorption.

The shock of seeing her like this, so soon after he had last seen her and held her alive, caused tears to flow copiously down his face; as if the image had physically and painfully struck him.

From somewhere far away, he heard the voice of the inspector. "Sir Roger, do you have any information which could throw any light on the death of this young woman?"

Wordlessly, Roger shook his head.

literary fiction from ROMAN Books

PIERRE FRÉHA

FRENCH SAHIB

What happens when a Frenchman falls in love with a young Indian guy? Set in India with a French protagonist, and written by a Frenchman, French Sahib is a French-Indian love story revealing the taboos of Indian society and the hypocrisies of French milieu. On his arrival in India Philippe is confronted with the traditional Indian values which are very unlikely from the country he hails from. When young Dipu wants to marry Philippe it is the stereotyped social values that become the stumbling block in their romance. How can they confront the unbridgeable gulf between the traditional East and the modern West? In *French Sahib* Pierre Fréha tells that amusing tale of identity, individuality, love and universal human need for connection and belonging.

Pierre Fréha was born in Algeria at the time when the country was a French colony. He has worked for many years as an independent, freelance writer. He visited and stayed in many countries including India. He is the author of two novels, one in English and the other in French. When not travelling, he lives in Paris.

Hardcover | £15.99 | $24.95
ISBN 978-93-80905-09-9
Available at your nearest bookstore

MINI NAIR

THE FOURTH PASSENGER

Set in Mumbai during the Hindu-Muslim conflict of the early 1990s, *The Fourth Passenger* is the story of four women raised with traditional Indian values, whose partnership give them the temerity to stand up against the religious extremism. Having reached their thirties and disillusioned with their lives and husbands, their decision to open an urban food stand is mingled with their memories of a distant past when two of them loved the same man. But, in order to establish their fledgling business, they must contend with individual temperament, extortionists, ruthless competitors, and most importantly, the prevailing religious intolerance.

Mini Nair has had two of her books published in India. A post graduate in chemistry, Mini Nair lives with her family and twin daughters in Mumbai where she was also born and brought up. *The Fourth Passenger* is her first novel.

Hardcover | £14.99 | $24.95
ISBN 978-93-80905-06-8
Available at your nearest bookstore

FIONA McCLEAN

FROM UNDER THE BED

Alice loves to paint pictures of fish. Her only problem is her addiction to cakes and pastries. To feed this obsession, she steals . . . and to rid herself of her spoils, she makes herself sick. Stick thin, Alice puts her fragile mind into the care of a psychiatrist, Professor Lucas, and tries to learn the rules people should live by. But her recovery soon brings a new and dangerous addiction—Brendan. As Alice struggles to cope with Brendan's violent outbursts, her dying father and poverty, she takes solace in her job at a massage parlour where she finds comfort with motherly Helen. But these are just temporary respites as her life with Brendan spirals downwards becoming a nightmarish maze.

Fiona McClean was born in Dusseldorf, Germany as the daughter of an army family. After studying Fine Arts at the University of Wales, Newport, she now lives the life of an accomplished painter in South France. Fiona loves to spend her time writing and painting, walking and horse riding. *From Under the Bed* is her debut novel.

Hardcover | £14.99 | $24.95
ISBN 978-93-80905-05-1
Available at your nearest bookstore